How Murder
Saved My Life

Dawn Merriman

Dedication

This book is dedicated to my loving husband, Kevin, who always supports me in all my crazy dreams. To my kids who have spent endless hours listening patiently to all my plans. To my sister, Angie, who always sees the best in me.

-Dawn Merriman

4

Prologue

He swung the board at her head. She ducked, the board grazing her shoulder. She ignored the pain. Her mind screamed run.

She didn't pause to grab clothes, just ran naked into the night.

The moonlight welcomed her. The fresh night air brushed her bare skin as she ran.

He followed her.

He swung again. The board scraped down her back as she fled.

She stumbled but kept running across the yard, into the woods.

He pursued.

Branches tore her bare skin, and weeds tangled her bare feet. Panic drove her, pushed her deeper into woods.

He stalked.

The brush closed in, tangled in her hair, catching her. She screamed, pulled, desperate to escape. The branch holding her hair broke away.

She turned to run, tripped, tumbled.

He pounced.

She scrambled, clawing at the dirt.

He caught her leg, flipped her on her back.

He stood over her, inspecting. "You shouldn't have run."

He raised the board again. She had no time to move away, no time to scream.

The board smashed her head in a swift arc.

White hot pain, then thankful oblivion.

Chapter 1

I have lived through my death many times.

A death of my own choosing.

It visits me nearly every night in my dreams.

The noose beckons to me, an old friend offering release. Pure and white, it gleams through the swirls of dust and fear in the barn. It waits for me, knowing I will lose to myself. The fence below it draws my bare feet forward in shuffles against rough concrete. I fight my feet, but they keep moving. Now to climb. Each step up pulls me closer to the oblivion I seek. My toes grip the top rail, struggle for balance. I hope to fall, to save myself. The tiny hope dwindles against the dark rising in me.

I reach for the noose, now my lifeline. Too worn to care it is a lie.

Do it. The voice says. *Make the pain go away.*

I whimper in response, lacking the strength to

fight anymore.

I slide the noose over my head in a smooth motion. The texture of the rope brushes against my skin in a soothing, familiar touch.

Just give in. Just give in.

My bare toes grip the wood of the fence, fighting of their own volition. They lose the battle, and I fall, the rope biting into my neck.

I jolt awake in a heavy sweat, instinctively reaching across the bed for my husband, Jackson. His warm body stirs, woken by my moans.

"Just a dream, Zoey," he says automatically, the way he does most mornings when he is still here when I wake. He pulls me close, my head on his chest. I focus on his heartbeat, the rhythmic sound chases the dream away. I breathe in his scent of sleep, a mixture of man sweat and remnants of his cologne. When I sleep alone, I often hold his dirty t-shirts to me, surround myself with this smell.

I am alive for now.

Jackson rubs my back, soothes me like a child. I cry against his chest. I don't want to die, I want to stay here with him. The voice has other plans.

Waking to nightmares doesn't surprise him anymore. Just part of being married to me I guess. He always holds me and calms me down, but he never asks what I see in them. I will never tell him, so better he doesn't ask.

If he knew the truth, he would stop loving you.

When I am clear minded, the voice sounds brutal, irrational. When I am dark-minded, I believe the lies.

The last few months, I have been getting better, making small steps of recovery from my depression. The closer I climb to better, the harder the voice fights to keep me down.

The noose draws closer, more inviting every time. Sometimes I see it when fully awake. I go out to the barn to do chores and imagine it hanging. It shimmers and calls to the dark part of my mind I desperately need to defeat but don't know how. The existence of the noose no longer terrifies me. The real terror is I am not afraid. The longing for it is my secret shame. The people I love would be hurt by the truth, so I hide it away. I force smiles and laughter to hide the pain.

I am awake now, and I don't want to think about it. I want to enjoy this moment with my husband. I am safe, for now.

Jackson senses I am calm now. His soothing hands begin to wander lower than my back. I giggle and push myself closer to his warm body.

"Since we are already awake," he teases. I welcome the distraction. My hands do some wandering of their own.

The alarm goes off, breaking our mood.

Jackson turns off the alarm and sighs at the lost opportunity.

"Where are you headed today?" I change the subject to the day ahead.

"Pittsburg. I will be back tomorrow night. A short run this time."

Jackson drives a semi-truck. He used to do short daily drives, came home to me and the kids each night. Now his job takes him away for days at a time. Not by choice, but by necessity.

Your fault. Your fault.

I block that train of thought as I often do. I hate Jackson being gone, but it's what we do now. The kids are away at school anyway.

Nothing to keep him home.

"What are you working on today?" he asks.

Jackson is on the road a lot, but I rarely leave our farm. I raise a small herd of KuneKune pigs, a specialty breed of pork to sell to restaurants and gourmet clients. My new bright idea venture that I hope will save us from financial ruin.

"I have to do the worming and vaccination shots on the new litter." I wish I had more to tell. I realize my day is much less important than his, and hate myself for it. I push that thought away as well. Plenty of time to think later.

"Why don't you wait until I get back and we can do them together?" he offers as he always does.

"Don't worry, I got it." Jackson wants to help, but it's my job, the least I can do.

We lay in silence a few more minutes, both of us aware we will be waking up alone tomorrow.

He sits on the side of the bed, stretches his neck. I reach across the bed, touch his thigh, not willing to let the sweet moment end. He squeezes my hand, then heads for the shower.

I toy with the idea of joining him in the shower, finish what we started, but know he will be really late then.

He doesn't expect me to get up with him, being so early, but I need coffee and a cigarette and time with him to chase the remaining shadows away. I leave our cocoon and pull on cutoffs and a t-shirt.

While he showers, I make the coffee and pack him some snacks and sandwiches in his small cooler. The cooler will ride with him in my place, full of my tokens of love. It's my way of being with him in some small way.

I let my pet pig, Allie, out of her night kennel. I give her a pat, and she hurries outside to do her business.

Jackson and I take our coffee to the garage, the door opens on a view of the first glimmers of the summer sunrise pouring over the northern Indiana fields. We have stools and a small table where we often sit together.

I light him a smoke and hand it to him, then light my own. I really should quit. Maybe tomorrow. Today the nicotine hits like a friend.

Jackson switches on the early morning farm report on the TV in the corner of the garage. The TV talks about crop prices, fertilizers, bigger better tractors. I never pay attention to it. I have my own ideas about farming, and they do not usually match up with mainstream practices. But I like sitting with Jackson, even this early in the morning. I watch his face as he looks at the TV.

Allie runs into the open garage, breaking into our quiet moment with her oinking.

Close behind her follows Denver, one of my KuneKune boars.

"Looks like he got out again," Jackson smiles at the large furry pig's sudden appearance.

"You little brat!" I laugh at my pig. Denver is a certified escape artist. All the other pigs in my small herd are content to stay where they belong. Denver likes to roam. I have never figured out how he escapes, we just find him wandering around every so often. I often wonder what people driving by think of a 300-pound pig roaming our yard.

"I'll help you put him back before I go."

Denver doesn't want to go back to his pasture, he'd rather root around in the garage and try out all the new smells. Allie is not impressed with his presence. He keeps trying to sniff her, she snaps back at him, even though he's more than twice her size.

I put Allie in the house, and Jackson helps me chase Denver out of the garage, towards the barn and the pastures.

Once out of the garage, Denver follows me.

"Pig, pig, treat!" I call to him. I have taught all my pigs to come to that command. A pig will do anything for a treat.

We walk as a trio through the morning damp grass, across the backyard to the barn, past the barn to the back pasture where my adult pigs live.

Denver stops to munch some grass here and there but otherwise follows until we reach the back pasture gate. He realizes where we have been leading him and isn't ready to go.

He runs past the gate and trots down the lane towards the woods.

"Denver, come back!"

He stops at my voice, looks back, deciding.

"Go grab some food. That should do it." I tell Jackson.

He hurries to the barn to get Denver a treat. I keep calling to the pig, trying to keep him from advancing down the lane. He has stopped but hasn't come back. He just stands in the lane, munching grasses he finds.

"Pig, pig, treat!" Jackson calls out, shaking the

feed bucket.

Denver lifts his head, definitely interested now. All the other pigs are interested too. They come running from the pasture to where we stand near the gate. Twenty plus pigs push against the gate and fence wanting a snack.

One ornery boar just stares at me from the lane.

Jackson and I look at each other. "Now what?" Usually, Denver isn't this naughty. I'm glad Jackson's here to help me.

I take the feed bucket from Jackson and throw a handful of pellets far over the fence. Most of the pigs go running for the food.

Denver moves closer, interested now that the others have something.

"You grab the gate," I say climbing the fence.

I keep tossing handfuls of food to the others, careful not to let them trample me. KuneKunes are very docile, but all pigs love food and can get carried away.

I don't look at Denver, but I hear him coming towards the fence. If his friends are eating, he wants some too. Jackson opens the gate and shoves it hard against Denver's rear as he enters the pasture.

Jackson has Denver contained, so I dump the rest of the bucket and climb back over the fence.

"We got him," I say and plant a quick kiss on

Jackson's cheek. "Thanks for your help."

"I didn't really do anything, but you're welcome." He kisses me back, not on my cheek.

The sun has climbed higher.

"I've got to go, babe," he says quietly.

My good mood vanishes. I wish he could stay and help me work on the farm. But he has to go.

In the house, he gathers his cooler of treats and his travel coffee mug I left on the kitchen table. I walk him to the door, yearning to make him stay, knowing he has to go. I am always amazed at his calm, surprised at his strength. I feel desperate, knowing the next few days will be lonely and dark especially after the lovely morning. I hate myself for needing him. I hate myself for making him have to go.

He holds me tight, kisses my hair. "That auction at the Applegate farm across the way is this weekend. Wanna go?" he asks.

"Absolutely." Plans for the weekend, yes!

"Good." Jackson turns to leave, and I want to snatch him back. He hesitates and meets my eyes. "Maybe you should go to lunch with your sister or something. Get out of the house for a while."

The dream must be on his mind, stewing in the background. He wants to protect me, but he can't. I can only protect myself.

For a moment, the idea of lunch with my sister sounds nice. Stephanie is always fun. Then the thought of sitting in a restaurant, surrounded by strangers, instantly makes my breath come in shorter bursts. I fight the un-natural panic.

"Yeah, maybe," I hedge. We both know I won't go. I rarely go anywhere. The only thing I hate more than the loneliness is venturing out into the world of people. It's not like I don't go anywhere, but normal social activities are hard for me. My anxiety attacks have ruined enough outings, it is easier just to stay home.

"I do have a therapy appointment tomorrow. So that's something." I give him what I hope is a convincing smile.

"Good. It will go well." His concern both touches and bothers me.

My need for therapy is one more failure. Expensive therapy drains our already dwindling bank account. I should be able to fix this monster in my head by myself. When the noose stopped scaring me, I chose to ask for help. After over 20 years of battling alone in silence, I tried therapy again.

"I really gotta go, babe. Smoochy kiss?" he asks, knowing it will make me laugh.

He squishes my cheeks together and kisses my pushed out lips. His hand cups my chin firmly. I will it to stay there.

We laugh together like we always do after a smoochy kiss. Then I release him to the world on the other side of our door.

The familiar voice starts its incessant hiss the moment Jackson leaves.

Your fault he left. If he loved you, he wouldn't leave you.

I hate the voice, my constant companion. While Jackson is home, it only whispers. When I am alone, it gets loud and relentless.

If you had done better, he wouldn't be going off to a job he hates. If you were better, you could fix this. You ruined his life, now fix it.

I lean against the closed door, begging the voice to stop.

I have been through this before. I can handle it. I have to.

"Get out of my head, this is God's house," I say out loud to the voice.

The evil doesn't like it when I fight back. It fights harder.

If he loved you, he wouldn't go. If you were smarter, you would have money. You idiot, you lost your business, and now your husband is gone, too.

The pain of loss, of guilt, of failure, crashes into me. It sneaks up and attacks, surprising me with its ferocity.

The weight of it buckles my knees, and I land crying on the floor, gasping for breath. I have been here before, too many times to count. I lay on the floor, try to concentrate on the dust I see on the rug, on the cobweb in the far corner, on the smell of coffee from the kitchen, anything other than the pain and guilt.

The rug beneath me is rough and solid beneath my cheek, beckoning me to hit my head on it.

If you hit just right, it won't leave a mark, no one will know. If you hit just right, the pain will focus, and you will feel better.

In the past, I would have given in, slammed my head.

I will not do it today. Like an addict, I count the days I have been "clean". I don't want to lose my streak. Giving in will start a downward spiral I don't think I can stop.

There are tools in the garage. You could do some nice things to your face.... Leave a mark so everyone can see what you truly are.

Chapter 2

Cutting and scarring my face is a new threat. The absolute terror of it snaps me back to the present.

"Use your skills from therapy," I sob out loud, begging my normal self for help.

"Breathing exercises. In for 4, hold for 4, out for 4." I walk myself through it, the way I learned. I speak out the words into the rug, giving them added strength. The extra oxygen in my blood cools the voice.

"Finger taps. Thumb to 1, thumb to 2..." I say the words aloud, focusing my attention on the movements.

Finally, the Lord's Prayer. "Our Father, who art in heaven..."

After the third time through the prayer, I have control again. I force myself off the rug, shaking with relief and pride. The attack had been unusually brutal, but I won.

"Get out of my head!" I yell through the empty house, my voice resonating strong and proud. It is *my* voice.

I dive for the tiny piglet. It manages to squirm

away from me in a flash of flying straw and squealing.

"Come here, you little stink!" Piglets are fast and don't like to be caught. This 7th and last one I have to give shots to today refuses to be caught. It started out as fun, but now I am ready to be done with it. It would certainly be an easier job with another pair of hands. But I can manage alone.

Luckily KuneKune momma pigs are well known to be calm even with babies. I can do what needs to be done right in their farrowing pens without having to worry about getting mauled to death. Regular farm pigs would be a different matter. Momma bears have nothing on protective momma pigs. Scarlet, the sow currently here with her babies, is super sweet so I can do what needs to be done without upsetting her. I just have to catch her last little bugger.

His tiny spotted body darts by me and I grab for a leg. Got it! I haul the squirmy guy up, settle him in my arms. "Shush now. Your littermates didn't give me this much trouble." He sinks into my arms and looks up at me with his dark, intelligent eyes. Kunes are just too cute. They have large furry ears and furry waddles hanging from either side of their chins. Their noses are short and sort of smooshed in. Plus, they will let me hold themususally. Once I can catch them, that is.

A quick jab of the needle in his rump makes him squeal the ear-rattling sound only a pig can make. I kiss him on the forehead and release him.

"All done for today, guys."

I sit in the pen with Scarlet and her littles. She flops her heavy body into the pile of clean straw, wiggles a bit until her belly is in the right position. The piglets know what to do and come running for breakfast, eager for momma after I chased them and stuck them with a needle. I rub her shaggy head and listen to her "sing" to the babies in rhythmic grunts. The piglets nose her belly, climb over each other, seeking their favorite teat. Their wild antics settle down, and they nurse, quiet at last. The serene scene enthralls me for several moments.

Juno snores behind me, in the other farrow pen where I put her this morning. I climb over the short wood fence of her enclosure and settle down beside her in the straw. Her belly is swollen with life. I rub her, and she grunts in sleepy satisfaction. I push gently just in front of her back leg. A tiny foot pushes back from the other side, making me smile. This miracle always amazes me. Little lives grow there, rolling and pushing, eager to join the world.

"Not much longer, Juno girl."

I climb out of the farrowing pens and put my shot supplies away. Our tractor and backhoe and collection of tools and implements fill most of the barn. This end houses the baby pens and the feed and supplies for the other pigs in the back pasture.

I sit on the feed bin, light a cigarette. Prickly hair rubs against my leg where I sit.

"Hey, Allie." I scratch my pet mini pig behind her ears. "Now that all the squealing's over you come to see what I am up to, huh?"

I kind of have a thing for pigs. My kids, Riley and Zack, call it an obsession. I don't mind the word, it fits. I grew up on a small traditional pig farm and fell in love with the things. Intelligent and sweet, with adorable little noses, I fell for them hard. A few years back I found out about "mini pigs" and had to have one. That's how I got Allie. The tiny black piglet with a white dot on her nose and white stocking feet easily wormed her way into my heart. Her attitude grew as quickly as she did. She roams the farm as her own private kingdom. She goes where she wants and does what she wants. I swear she struts along the fences of the other pigs and taunts them.

"I own this farm. Bow to your queen. You poor peasant pigs have to stay behind the fences, and I do what I want." Never mind that what she usually wants to do is doze in the sun, or lounge in her baby pool. I've never seen a more spoiled pig or a better friend. A near constant shadow she follows as I move around doing chores or working on projects. I don't know what I would do without her, especially now the kids are off at college and Jackson is away so much. Allie helps me keep what little sanity I have left.

"What you want to work on next?" I ask her.

As an answer, she flops onto her side so I can rub her belly, all 100 plus pounds of her.

"Yeah, I know how you feel. Too hot to do much today." I rub her belly absently. With all the usual chores done, I have a few hours ahead to fill with busy work. My previous life whirled by in a blur of quickly growing children, divorce at 34, meeting Jackson, blending our new family of Riley and Zack and Jackson's daughter, Allison.

Behind it all, keeping me grounded, was my business. The beautiful business I created from nothing. In my previous life, I designed clothes. Hard to believe now as I sit in cutoffs and a smeared t-shirt. My short curls need cut and haven't even seen a brush today. I hardly look like the clothing designer type. But once upon a time that's what I did. Once, I had more than 10 employees sewing my designs and an assistant to help with the tedious office work, leaving me to the creation of my dresses. Once I had clothes hanging in several small boutiques and a thriving online store. Once I had a purpose and a big paycheck. The money came easy, maybe too easy. So easy in fact, I convinced Jackson to quit his job and join me on my crazy journey. So proud and full of myself, I believed I could pay all the bills, could carry us on my dream.

I forgot life doesn't work that way. Trends change. Sales drop. The money becomes harder to make. Scrambling to survive the downturn, I scraped and clawed. I still failed. My employees were laid off and no longer wanted to talk to me. With no money for the rent, I was forced to move out of my lovely shop where my designs came to life. Stores stopped carrying my dresses. Online orders dried up. Within a year, my company disappeared. Twelve years of climbing and then a steep drop.

The speed of it still shocks me. It died so quickly. I had built it from nothing, and I should be proud. Instead, I am ashamed. A thick, bone-chilling shame of failure. I was supposed to be someone. We were going to take the world by storm. The storm swallowed us up instead.

Bills don't care about dreams or storms or hopes. Bills need to be paid. So Jackson now drives a truck again. No more short runs and home every night. Now he drives long hauls, for better money. I had promised security, vacations, new cars, a happy life. The reality for him is a hard seat, miles of road and rarely coming home.

The reality for me is failure and guilt.

You've ruined his life. Now you think this new gourmet pork venture will fix things? You will fail at this the way you failed before.

I push the voice away. A famous TV preacher I like to watch says God has a plan for my life. Dark times like these are tests. If I have faith, he will bring me through. I can only hope he is right. For now, I am tired of thinking about it.

"Come on, Allie. Time for lunch. I have book work to do anyway." I swear the pig understands English. She hops up in a huff, hoping lunch means for her.

I fill my day with mindless bookwork, evening chores, and nighttime TV. After three episodes of true-crime shows, I need a break. I turn off the TV. I like watching crime shows. No matter how bad a day I'm having, I'm better off than the people on those shows. It makes me miss my kids, especially Riley, my daughter. I suppose every mother worries their daughter will fall victim to a predator. She's far way in Costa Rica right now, I can't protect her from here.

I try to call Riley but only get voice mail.

I try her twin brother Zack instead. He answers.

"Hey, there's my handsome son," I can hear

the smile in my voice. I can always manage a smile for my kids. It's easy and natural.

"Moommmaaa," he sings to me as they do in Bohemian Rhapsody by Queen. He has done this since middle school. The nostalgia of it pulls at my heart.

"How's it going, baby doll? Learning all the engineering in the world?"

"Yeah, something like that. These summer classes are keeping me busy. You got lucky catching me. I just finished a project and heading out with the guys to relax a bit." He breaks into a laugh, "I'm coming. Give me a minute," he says to a friend in the room with him. "Mom, I gotta go."

"Okay, love. I wanted to hear your voice, and now I have," I say with forced nonchalance, secretly jealous of his friends.

Zack pauses. He knows when I'm off, even when I cover it well.

"You doing okay?"

"Of course. You know me, I'm always okay."

Liar.

"Knock it off, I said I'm coming," he says to the room. I feel guilty for keeping him from his fun. "You sure, Mom? You sound down."

"I'm fine. Go have fun. Talk to you in a few days. Love you, bye."

"Love you, bye." We end every phone call the

same way. You never know the last time you will talk to someone.

I hang up the phone and sink into the silence of the living room. The only sounds are the aquarium bubbling in the corner and Allie snoring where she sleeps on the floor next to the couch. I think about the voices brutal attack this morning. I don't want to live like this forever. I don't want to live in fear of the world and myself.

"This is stupid!" I suddenly yell at the room, startling Allie awake. I have to get out. I have to see anything other than the inside of my house.

I grab my truck keys, a soda, and my smokes and hit the road. I want to drive.

Chapter 3

The dark fields lay sleeping under the summer night. They stretch lazily on either side of the road, broken occasionally by hulks of houses shrouded in trees. A few porch lights are on here and there, but mostly the countryside sleeps. I am alone in the dark, the way I like it.

Music blares from my radio, smoke trails out the window as I light another. I have no destination, I just don't want to go home to the empty house. So I drive.

Preoccupied with my own thoughts and singing at the top of my lungs along with the radio, I almost don't see the car half in a ditch. Very few people are out on the county roads after midnight. I slow down, careful to avoid the car as I pass, assuming it's deserted and left for the morning.

I see her. A small blonde woman stands by the trunk, obviously upset and confused about how to get out. Sitting in my truck, I can tell she's not a country girl. The fancy car, platinum hair and general air of "what now" gives her away.

My first instinct is to keep driving. I don't like strangers. I have seen enough crime shows and Dateline episodes to know danger comes in all forms, even pretty blonds. She looks up at me as I drive past. The look on the young woman's face makes me stop.

I park in the dark, take a deep breath and climb out.

"Looks like you're stuck," I approach her car awkwardly.

"Thank you for stopping. I've been here for ages. I slid off the road, and I can't get back out. Can you help me?" The young woman pulls on her shirt, follows me on stiff legs.

In answer, I use my cell phone flashlight and check out the situation. Dirt and stones are thrown in spattered tracks behind the rear wheels. Apparently, she had tried several times to power her way out. City mistake.

"I would call my husband, but we got in a fight, and I stormed out. I don't want to call him. You know how it is." She squats next to me, looks at her tires deep in the dirt. "I don't want to ask for his help after I made such a big scene leaving and all. Lord what a mess! I had no idea what to do. I don't even know who to call for a tow truck."

"I have a tow rope in my SUV. I can get you out." I walk to the back of my truck, she follows like a scared puppy.

"I about gave up and started walking back. Then you pulled up. It hasn't been fun standing here in the dark on this back road wherever we are."

Her torrent of words pours over me. Not used to so much talk all at once, I just look at her and blink.

"I was getting so scared. That's silly, nothing out here but corn, but you know. I'm not used to the country. I'm Becca Trenton, by the way." She offers me her hand.

"Zoey DiMeo." I like shaking hands, you can tell a lot about a person that way. Her handshake is surprisingly firm, despite her scared child manner. I like her better instantly. "Don't worry, Becca. I can get you out. We've done it lots of times."

"We?" she looks around, expecting to see someone with us.

"My husband and I. That's why I keep a tow rope in the truck. People are always running into trouble out here, and Jackson likes helping them out." I don't tell her this is the first time I have helped someone by myself.

"That's so cool. Wow, thank you so much. I don't know what I was going to do. Plus I just got my nails done, and I don't want to mess them up. See, they're American flags. You know, for the Fourth of July. Aren't they great?" She shows me her hands, looking for approval.

Her nails? Seriously? Definitely not from around here.

"Nice." I squat to attach the tow rope to the rear of her car while Becca talks non-stop. I wish I had just driven by, but I need to go out of my comfort zone and interact with people. This counts.

"I'm from Chicago. Although I did spend one summer here at my grandparent's place a long time ago."

She pauses, I feel like I should say something.

"Oh yeah," I manage as I hook the other end to the trailer hitch on my truck.

"Yeah, that was like 10 years ago. They lived in that big old farmhouse on Six Mile Rd. Do you know the one? You know it has all those porches and the huge barns. It's quite a place."

I stand and face her. "The Applegate arm, where the auction is this weekend? Zeke and Lydia were your grandparents?"

"Grandma died a few years back, and Grandpa passed last month. Did you know them?"

"Not personally. But you know how everyone knows everyone here in Sugartree. They seemed to be nice people."

"I hadn't seen them in a long time. But Grandma and Grandpa were always nice to me, you know. The place belongs to me now, I guess. We're having the auction this weekend to get rid of all the furniture and farm stuff."

"I've always been jealous of that farm. What're you going to do with the house and land? Gotta be at least 100 acres there." I lean against her car.

"I don't know anything about farms, or acres or any of that. I haven't been here for 10 years. Ricky and I just came down for a few days to be here for the auction." She runs her hand through her long hair then leans against the car close to me. I resist the urge to slide away from her. She obviously needs to talk. "Of course, now Ricky's all pissed off. But, he's always pissed off, the jerk. He wants me to sell the property. He's like 'Do you know how much money we can make off this old place?' All he thinks about is money." She leans her head back and looks up at the stars. Her pretty face looks younger than the mid-twenties she actually is. We stand quietly for a moment, looking at the stars spread above us. No sound except the wind through the corn. No other cars have passed this whole time. It's just the two of us in the night.

"I don't know if I want to sell it or not. I thought I did, but once we got here, I wasn't sure.

Like, I don't have to decide right now, right? It's not going anywhere, why rush into it? Maybe I want to keep it. Maybe I will become a farmer. Who knows, right?"

Wow, she talks fast.

"There's no reason to rush into anything. You can sell later," I shrug.

"Exactly what I said. Does Ricky see it that way? No of course not. As always, he just wants what he wants. Who cares what I want, you know." She looks at me for confirmation.

"Men," I offer. This whole conversation feels bizarre to me. Who talks like this to a complete stranger? The intimacy is uncomfortable.

Not sure what else to do, I get back to pulling her out of the ditch. "Get in your car, and when I tell you, put it in reverse. Don't give it too much gas, just enough to help me pull."

She looks concerned.

"It's easy. I will be doing most of the work. Just don't run into me."

I remember having this exact conversation with Zack when he got stuck in a ditch the first time. He had that same anxious look Becca has now. "It will be fine."

I put my truck in 4-wheel drive, slowly creep forward. The tow rope tightens, holding me still for a moment, then we move forward again. Just like that, she's out of the ditch.

"You did it!" she jumps out of her car and runs over to me.

Afraid she will throw her arms around me, I bend down and unhook my tow rope. "You're good to go, now."

She continues on with her previous train of thought. "Maybe I'm not being fair. I mean, Ricky has a point. The farm's worth a lot of money. We would be set. He can be a jerk, but he can be sweet too, you know. He's waiting for me, probably worried. I've been gone a long time."

Becca starts looking around, trying to determine which way to take home. Her quick change of heart confuses me.

"Go down that way to the next stop sign and turn right. You aren't as lost as you thought." I close the SUV hatch. I am ready to go home myself.

"Man, I can't thank you enough. Zoey, was it? Thanks, Zoey. I don't know what I would have done if you hadn't stopped. Sit here til Ricky came to find me? But we only have the one car with us, so not sure how he would have been able to do that."

Becca moves to give me a hug. The bubbly young blonde has kind of grown on me, so I allow it this time. Her tiny frame clings to me a moment longer than necessary. I smell the perfume in her hair, sweet and airy like her personality. She reminds me of my kids, and I like feeling needed.

"I didn't do much, but you're welcome." I release her and step away. "Look, don't be too hard on Ricky. This is all new to him too." I walk her to her car door, suddenly hesitant to let her go.

"I know." She climbs into her car, anxious to get home now.

"Just get through the auction and give it time. If you decide to sell, I know you won't have any trouble finding a buyer. It's a very nice farm, lots of people want it. Heck, I would buy it if I could. It backs to my property."

"Really, so we're, like, neighbors? How cool! I barely know anyone here."

"Well, now you do." I smile at her and give her hood two soft taps, the country signal for good-bye.

Chapter 4

"Hey, Zoey. Good to see you." Janey, my therapist, croons as we take our seats in her office. She always starts like this. I secretly wonder if her pleasure is real, or something she says to all her clients.

She seems sincere. I choose to believe she's happy to see me.

"How have the last few weeks gone?" Janey settles her notebook in her lap as we start. I would give anything to read her notes.

I hesitate, not sure how much I want to reveal. After twenty some years, my depression and anxiety have woven so far into who I am, I don't know what I should fear. I stare at my uncomfortable shoes instead of answering.

Janey watches me quietly, letting me settle in, letting me lead. Sometimes I get the feeling she can see right through me. I can smile and seem chipper, but she knows the truth. Not her first day on the job.

"Not great, but not too awful," I hedge. I flick my eyes at the window, watch the leaves flutter on the tree. I want to be outside, not here.

Keep your mouth shut.

"Are the new meds helping?"

Over the years, I have tried numerous medications for my depression and anxiety. Nothing helped, some made them worse. Janey convinced me to have the genetic testing done to see what meds might work and which ones are not a good fit for me. Turned out all the ones I had tried were on the "do not take" part of my profile. The new medication has shown some promise. At least I'm not hurting myself anymore.

"Some." I keep staring at the tree outside.

"How are the pigs?" she knows this will at least get me talking.

"The pigs are good." Glad to have something safe to talk about. "I have a new litter, so my total herd's up to 30 some now. Another litter due next week. In another few months, I will have some ready to butcher finally." I babble on for a while about my pig business. My eyes dart to the clock as the minutes tick by. I know I'm wasting time, wasting money, but I'm afraid to talk about anything else. After a few minutes, I stop, stare back at my shoes.

"I'm glad your new business is going well. But how are *you* doing?" Janey uncrosses her legs, unconsciously leans forward, eager for me to talk.

This question always baffles me. I don't know how to separate myself from my businesses. Logically, I know they should be different things. Emotionally, they are the same thing to me.

"I'm doing okay, all things considered," I evade again. "Jackson's on a run until tomorrow, so the farm's pretty quiet right now. The kids are great. Riley's doing a semester abroad studying eco-architecture in Costa Rica of all places. Zack's still at Purdue doing a summer semester trying to graduate early. Allison's still out in New Mexico in the Air Force. I wish they had come home for the summer, but they're out conquering the world." The pride drips from my words, mixed with longing.

"I miss them." I bow my head.

Crap. Janey barely said anything but broke through the armor I struggle to keep on at all times. Tears come unwanted, my chest clamps in pain.

"I should be used to the kids not being home. They're not really gone, just off at college and now taking extra summer classes. But I miss them." I rub my palms down my shorts, an unconscious soothing motion.

All moms miss their kids when they go off to school. You're not special.

I stare at a picture on the wall, not really seeing it. Janey scratches notes on her pad.

"It's like I have no purpose anymore. First I lose the business, then I lose my kids. I know I have the new business, but..." I don't know how to finish the sentence, so I sit in silence as tears scald down my cheeks.

Janey gently hands me the box of tissues. "You have lost a lot. It's normal to feel confused."

"I have so much to be thankful for, and I am thankful. I don't understand why I'm so unhappy. I should be happy. I have a wonderful life anyone would want, so why can't I be happy? Or at least less miserable."

You're an idiot. You stupid loser. Do you think she has nothing better to do than listen to you whine? You will never be happy.

The voice rages so loudly, I'm surprised Janey can't hear it and continues with her train of thought.

"Zoey, you have to allow yourself to grieve the loss of your business. It was important to you, and it's gone. You have to face the loss, not hide from it in guilt."

"I have destroyed our lives, and I don't know what to do about it. I don't know how to fix it." I say this every time. The litany has lost all meaning. At the same time, it's attached to my core.

"You have not destroyed your life. There's nothing you need to fix." This litany has no meaning to me either.

Oh, you know you did destroy it. You weren't smart enough. not creative enough. If you had worked harder, made better designs, better decisions, you wouldn't be such a mess. If you give in, this can all go away.

I nod to Janey like I'm supposed to.

"But we're broke. Nearly every day I have to check the bank account. I have to move money around to make sure everything gets paid. It's a constant worry. What if he tries to buy something on the road and the card gets declined? What if I leave him halfway across the country with no money? What if he finds out how bad off we really are?" I gasp in air, my ears ring. I have not said these fears out loud before.

"What if that happens?" Janey's soft voice leads me.

"He will know," I choke out, defeated. "He will know I don't have it all together."

"So what if he knows? He's a grown man. You don't need to protect him. You two are a team, in this together. " She leans forward in her seat, excited I am finally hearing what she has known all along.

"Put yourself in his place," she says.

I close my eyes, and I picture Jackson far away out in the world, wanting to be home, but sacrificing for his family. His broad shoulders fill

41

the truck seat. His capable hands guide the massive truck expertly. His heavy jaw set in quiet strength. I know she means his place emotionally. Instead, I picture him physically. It's easier that way.

"He needs you to be his wife, not his shield. You can't do this alone and he can't either. You have to be honest with him."

"What if he hates me once he knows?" The fundamental truth, the central fear I have never let surface.

"He loves you for all that you are *and* all that you're not, Zoey. Trust him, trust in his love. Do you have so little faith in him?"

"I believe in Jackson more than I have believed in anyone."

"There you go. Hold on to that. It has been two years since all this happened. Are you ever going to be able to forgive yourself and move forward?"

I take a deep breath before I answer, happy for the slight change of tactic. The sun shines in her office window and on my leg. It seems brighter than it was earlier.

"I want to. This is our life. I should enjoy it while I'm still here. Then other times the dark voice wins. I'm so tired of it all."

Something in my words catches her attention. Her eyes sharpen.

You better watch out. She will figure out your

secret.

"The voice is still loud? What does it say?"

"The usual. You suck. It's your fault. Why are you even here, you stupid loser? Stuff like that. It's relentless. I can't make it stop."

You can make it stop. I have shown you how to sink into oblivion and end the pain.

Janey makes more notes, waits for me to decide if I want to explain. I think about yesterday morning on the floor. I choose to tell her. I can't get better if I'm not honest.

"I had an especially bad morning yesterday," I start.

"Bad how?"

"Do you believe in the devil?" My question surprises her.

"I believe in God, as you know. So I suppose I believe in the devil, too."

"It's like the devil lives in my head. He is the voice. I have been getting better, and he doesn't like it. When I fight one threat, he throws a worse threat at me."

"That's interesting. What do you mean?" Frequently Janey asks questions she already knows the answer to. This time, she's genuinely curious.

"I had an especially bad morning yesterday. I woke with the usual nightmare. And then Jackson had to leave. Suddenly a wave of guilt and fear and self-hatred rushed in so strong it knocked me to the floor. The voice wanted me to hit my head on the floor. I refused to do it."

"That's good," Janey says gently, not sure where I'm going with this story.

"The voice got mad. It told me to go get a tool and cut my face. Leave a scar, so everyone will know how bad I am." I am amazed at myself for saying the words out loud. I never share the darkest thoughts, not even with Janey.

I expect her to cringe away from me in disgust, appalled at my depravity.

"I am so sorry you had to suffer through that," she says instead. The words are not empty motions. The genuine empathy nearly breaks me.

"I didn't hurt myself. I did the steps. I got myself through it."

"You won," she says simply. "A few months ago, you might not have been able to resist the temptation. You're really making progress. You do see the progress, right?"

"I do see it, and it feels good. It's just…." I'm not sure I should go on, how to say it without sounding hokey. "It's like there's a battle for my soul, good and evil, in my head. The more I get better, the harder the devil tries to win. I wish the devil would just give up and leave me alone."

"Only God can win that battle, Zoey. You have to trust him enough to let him fight for you. You can't do this by yourself."

"Let God fight for me. I like that. I need all the help I can get." Janey and I have never discussed things in this way before. I like the change.

"How are the nightmares?" Janey pushes on.

The noose flashes into my mind. Janey knows I am having nightmares, but not that I kill myself in them. My good feeling vanishes.

If you tell her the truth, she will be forced to call the authorities on you. You won't be able to walk out of here. You will be locked up in a padded cell so you can't hurt yourself. You want to really ruin your life, then tell her. I dare you.

I am not ready to have that conversation yet. Yesterday morning's battle and the discussion about Jackson is all I can face right now.

"It's nearly every day now. It's like I am being crushed by the pressure of life and smothered with worry." Not entirely the truth, but not untrue either. "It's not a great way to start the day."

"What would be a better way to start your day?" Ah, Janey and her open-ended questions.

"No nightmares would be nice. Sometimes I start with saying 'This is the day the Lord has made. Let us rejoice and be glad in it.' That helps set a better tone."

"That's a good idea. Anything else?" I don't want to talk about the dream and what it represents.

45

"Jackson and I are going to an auction this weekend," I say instead. She sees through the awkward attempt to change the subject, but she allows it. I have made good progress finally. I deserve some happy talk.

"That sounds fun."

"I love auctions. It's one of the few things we do for fun together."

"And how will you do with the crowd? Do you have a plan if the anxiety comes?"

Only a loser like you needs a plan to go out and do something.

"Some crowds don't bother me, especially when I am having fun. I don't think about it too much. Plus I have the tricks you taught me." Oh, social anxiety is so much fun. How did I get to this? I used to be able to go out and do things like everyone else. Now, leaving the farm is a whole adventure. I do fine at the things I'm used to, gas station, grocery, feed mill, stores. A few humiliating panic attacks in public places makes it easier to stay home and hide from anything unfamiliar.

"That's great. It will do you good to practice being out."

"I know. I really need to push out of my comfort zone more." Just saying the words makes my heart beat faster.

"I did meet a new person last night." I offer.

46

"Oh, yeah?"

"I pulled a young woman's car out of a ditch. She was nice." It's not much, but I want to prove I'm making progress.

Janey smiles. "You pulled her out of a ditch? Most people can't do that."

I shrug. My sister is always telling me the stuff we do on the farm is interesting. It's just daily life to me.

"I had to get out of the house. So I went for a drive and found her needing help. You're always telling me to try new things."

"I'm proud of you. You are getting better, Zoey. It just takes time."

Thankfully, the voice doesn't say anything. That's a good sign.

Chapter 5

"I hope you get to meet Becca today," I tell Jackson as we drive to the auction, excitement sparking my words. "She talks a lot, but she's nice."

"Glad you met someone new." He squeezes my hand. "Maybe you two can be friends if she decides to stay on."

"That could be nice." I haven't had a friend for a long time. I thought the women who worked for me were friends. I enjoyed the conversations about our lives and the daily chatter that naturally happens in an office. As soon as I had to lay them off one by one, I learned the difference between friend and employee. Another thing I got wrong.

"She will be in a hurry to get back to Chicago, but it might be nice practice to be friendly while she's here." I'm not used to this excitement, and welcome the change.

I squeeze Jackson's hand as we drive and lean over and give him a kiss on the cheek. It's auction day!

"Wow, what a turnout!" Jackson exclaims. Vehicles are parked in a long line down the road.

A section of a field has been set up for parking but is already full. "We should have walked through the back property to get here. It would have been closer," he jokes.

"The exercise will do us good," I joke back.

The auction has already started. The call of the auctioneer cries over the crowd of people and cars in a staccato of numbers and words. The excitement thrums through me as we get our bidder numbers. People mill about expectantly, looking over the items for sale. An air of anticipation winds around the crowd mixed with the scent of popcorn and hot dogs cooking.

Jackson and I enter the vast tent and wander among the tables of items for sale. We mostly come for fun, but we usually end up with something. We typically take home an old tool, or antique item we think looks cool. This old farm overflows with great stuff. It's going to be hard to settle on one thing.

"DiMeo, good to see you," a voice cuts into our happy bubble.

Bernard Traiger. Ugh! The short man waddles over to us. His massive belly strains against the buttons of his expensive shirt. A thick gold watch jangles on his wrist. Jackson and I have joked before that he wears it loose so it will rattle and draw attention.

Traiger practically owns half of the town of

Sugartree. He owns the building I rented for my shop. He was livid when I had to break my lease. "Should have known better than to rent to a woman," he'd said. Never mind I had paid the rent on time for years. The humiliation of that meeting still rankles.

Despite his general dislike of me, Traiger is friendly with Jackson. Jackson has that effect on people. Everyone likes him.

The men shake hands. Traiger barely looks my way. Fine with me. I'd rather pretend he wasn't there.

"Traiger, surprised to see you here. Didn't know you were the auction going type." I smile, reading between Jackson's words. Everyone knows Traiger only buys the most expensive things. No way he came to buy a piece of used furniture or an old mower.

"Gotta slum it sometimes," he laughs. "I'm here to check out the property. Rumor has it this farm is for sale." Oh no. Traiger as a neighbor?

"I don't think she's decided yet," I pipe in. Traiger looks at me, shocked I have opened my mouth when the men are talking.

"We'll see about that. My attorney said a young city girl inherited the property. She has no business owning a farm like this." The thought of Becca going up against this man in a business deal makes me cringe. Of course, she might talk him to death and win.

Annoyed with the man, I shrug and turn my attention to the auctioneer. Jackson finishes his conversation and joins me, standing close.

"I don't know how you can stand to talk to that guy," I say.

"Oh, he's not so bad. Besides, better to be friendly with the lord of the manner, since we're just peasants here in the slums," he laughs. The little joke breaks the tension, and I lean against him.

"You know he's had a rough time since his daughter disappeared."

"He was a jerk long before then." Still, I feel sorry for him. When Cammie Traiger vanished years ago, it was all over the news, the biggest thing to happen in Sugartree. They never found her. Most people, including me, figured she took off to get away from her father.

There were rumors Traiger killed his daughter and got away with it. I don't like the man, but I can't imagine he could kill his own child. The rumors nearly ruined him, but they also drove him to succeed. He became even more ruthless in his business dealings.

"Forget him. Let's finish looking around. They're going to be on the kitchen stuff for a while."

We pore over the items, searching for the

treasures buried among the overflow. Jackson has a good eye. We often play a game at auctions, try to guess what price something will sell at. My predictions are often way off. Jackson's usually dead on. He grew up going to auctions, has an instinct for it.

"Look at this, an old set of 'Little House on the Prairie' books. The whole set." I nearly bounce as I show Jackson the books. My favorite show growing up, I love the "Little House" series. I already own all the books, but this set is old, not first edition, but old and interesting. I look at Jackson expectantly.

"If you want it."

"It will probably go for nothing. It's mixed in with all these old papers and stuff. Mostly a box of junk and some old comic books."

"You just jinxed yourself." He smiles. If I think it will go for nothing, it usually goes high.

We stand around for nearly an hour, watching the auction, playing our price game. Jackson's winning of course. They're still several tables away from the books I want.

"I'm gonna take a bathroom break. Can you watch my box?" I ask.

"Sure," he replies absently. The auctioneer is

selling old tools, a personal favorite of his.

The Port-a-John sits back away from the tent and people, next to one of the smaller barns. Using the Port-a-John sucks, but it's better than squatting in a field.

I hurry to do my business while holding my breath against the strong chemical smell. As I zip up my shorts, I hear voices outside.

"I told you I haven't made a decision yet. Now stop asking me." It's Becca. I may have just met her, but I have heard enough words come from her mouth to be able to recognize her voice. I haven't seen her yet today.

"You don't know what you're doing, little miss." I recognize Traiger's rough voice as he bullies her.

"Don't, 'Little Miss' me. I haven't made a decision yet, but I do know what I'm doing. I'm from Chicago, you know." She struggles to act tough, but I hear the uncertainty behind her words. Traiger hears it too.

"You're a long way from Chicago. Listen, I have been working on buying this property from your grandfather, Zeke, for years now. We had a verbal agreement, all we needed was the paperwork. Then he goes and dies and leaves it all to you. I'm out thousands of dollars in surveys and soil samples. This property should be mine already."

"What if I don't want to sell?" Becca's voice wavers.

"You have no choice. I will get this property one way or another. You're in over your head here. I own this town, and I don't back down."

"Is that a threat?"

"Take it as you want, but I will have this property."

Traiger storms off and I hear Becca sniffle. I wait, hoping she will walk away, not wanting her to know I overheard. She keeps sniffling. My protective instinct kicks in, and I exit the Port-a-John.

Becca physically jumps when she sees me and swipes at her tears.

"Zoey, it's just you."

"Sorry, I overheard you two. Traiger's such a jerk."

"Do you know him?"

"Everyone knows him. He thinks he's king of Sugartree."

Becca stares at the ground.

"Are you okay?" I step closer.

"It's been an awful day. I didn't think selling all my grandparent's stuff would be so hard. I have so many great memories of them from the summer I stayed here. I wasn't close to my grandparent's the last few years, you know how it is."

"It must be hard," I offer.

"Guess it's hitting me they're gone. I lost my parents a few years ago, and grandma and grandpa were the only family I had left. They left me the farm, no one else to leave it to."

Becca stares at the crowd near the tent.

"Now this Traiger guy thinks it's his. It's a lot to take in, you know. Like, what am I supposed to think? What am I supposed to do? Ricky's still being a jerk about it too. Why can't everyone leave me alone?"

In frustration, Becca pushes her long blond hair away from her face, her flag painted nails glinting in the sun. She tucks a strand behind her ear, exposing a bruise high on her cheekbone. I lock eyes on the mark, and she quickly moves her hair back to cover it.

I raise my eyebrows in question, fury lighting my gut.

"It's nothing." She fidgets with her hair, looks away.

I wait for her to continue, instead of replying. A trick I've learned as a mom. It works.

"Ricky didn't believe me about being stuck in a ditch. He was sure I was out with some other guy. I told him I only know one person in this town, and I definitely don't want to see him. Ricky didn't believe me. He got carried away, that's all." She looks away, her small shoulders

56

slumped.

"Becca, you…."

"Seriously, Zoey, it's nothing." She interrupts. She straightens her back and lifts her chin. "Enough of that stuff. Are you having a good time at the auction?"

I want to press her about the bruise, but I barely know her.

It's none of your business, stay out of it, loser.

"I'm having a great time. My husband, Jackson, is here. We're waiting to bid on a set of old 'Little House' books."

"Oh, my gosh, those were mine! I forgot all about them. Grandma gave them to me. They were a great read while I was here that summer. A little young for me, but I loved them anyway. I thought someday I could be a writer like Laura Ingalls. I started keeping a 'remembrance book,' you know. Like Laura did. The silly things a 15-year-old girl does."

"I love them, too. Do you want to come watch the auction and meet Jackson? He's watching the box, so we don't miss it."

Becca doesn't answer, her attention held by someone in the crowd. I follow her gaze, but nothing stands out.

"Becca?" Her face is pale, her eyes far away.

"If you don't mind, I'd rather go inside." She starts towards the house, eager to be away. "It's been a long day. Anyway, Ricky's watching TV. This whole auction annoys him. I should go make sure he is all right." She hurries away from the auction and back to the house.

I want to make her come with me, but let her go.

"I was starting to think you got lost," Jackson says when I finally make it back to him. "They're almost up to your books."

"Oh, good I didn't miss it. I ran into Becca. I will tell you about it later."

"Don't look now, but Carter Bays is checking out your book box."

Carter Bays regularly goes to the auctions so we see him around. I don't like people as a general rule, especially scrawny guys with wild eyes. He buys a lot of stuff to re-sell, but I don't think he sells much of what he buys. He lives in a run-down crappy little house next to this farm. He spends a lot of his free time shooting guns on the back of his property. It echoes across our land annoying me. I worry a stray bullet will accidentally hit one of my pigs in the back pasture.

"That scrawny kid's not getting my books."

The bidding finally starts on the box. I like to wait until the auctioneer gets down as low as possible before jumping in. Only an amateur bids at the first number offered.

At $2, I yep loudly. Most people raise their hand or their bidder card. I like to yep. It usually catches people off guard, and I can win the bid.

The bid goes to $3, I don't see who outbids me.

$4, yep.

I lose the bid at $5, yep it back at $6. Lose it at $7.

"Who's bidding against me?" I ask Jackson.

"Carter. Told you he wanted that box. He's probably after the comics."

"Ten dollars!" I yell. Jumping bids like that is another tactic that usually scares people off.

I lose the bid at $11.

"Fifteen dollars!"

Carter turns and glares at me.

"Wow, you ticked him off," Jackson chuckles, he loves a good auction battle.

The auctioneer is doing his ending bit, raising his voice in question, asking for any last bids. Carter keeps staring at me full of anger. At the last moment, he realizes what's happening and turns to bid.

"Sold!" The auctioneer says. Too late for him. The books are mine.

Carter stomps towards me as Jackson goes forward to collect the box.

"I wanted that box," Carter hisses.

"You should have kept bidding," I quip, having fun.

Carter stares at me, his eyes snapping.

"It's just a box, Carter. No friends at an auction, you know." I keep my tone light, confused by his anger.

Jackson walks up, box in hand.

Carter looks at the box, then at Jackson. He turns and storms out of the tent.

I take the box from Jackson. "Some people don't know how to have fun."

Chapter 6

Beginning the day with little squirmy bodies and tiny squished noses sets a tone of hope for my day. I always start chores in the farrowing house so I can visit the babies.

My sow, Scarlet, shoots me a look that seems to say, these kids are driving me nuts, but aren't they great. I recognize that look from human moms too. I give the sows their feed and a pat behind the ears.

"Sorry, kid. A few more weeks and you can go back to the big pasture with your friends," I tell Scarlet.

I wander into the main barnyard, Allie as my constant companion. The early morning July sun beats down on the gravel, the heat travels into my bare feet. I rarely wear shoes at the farm. I like to feel the earth below me, the energy of the planet on my soles.

A breeze rattles through the ancient cottonwood trees nearby. The sound of the shaking leaves blocks out the world. The lonely sound condenses the universe to this spot. Nothing exists beyond the sound. Nothing exists besides Allie and me, alone in the barnyard, and the dry bone rattle of the leaves.

If you are all alone, why be here? Who would miss you if you were gone?

I never want to hear it. I shake my head, physically pushing the thoughts away. The long day stretches before me. Hours to fill. A chill crawls unbidden across my shoulders.

"Come on, Allie. The back pasture pigs will think they're starving by now." I need to distract myself. I need to move away from the sound.

As soon as they see me coming, the squeals of the pigs peal through the air. Pigs like food and they're not shy in their demands.

Allie snorts, bothered, hesitant. Normally, she trots along in anticipation, wants her share of the food knowing full well she already ate. Today she drags behind, a low moan of distress seeping from her round body.

"What's your deal?" She often senses my mood, and I am out of sorts today.

More than twenty pigs live in this pasture. My gourmet butcher hogs grow up in sunshine and green grass. They sleep under the stars and in pig huts that dot the field. Near the back of their pasture, a section of woods and brush gives them shade. I know each pig by name and shout greetings as they run to the fence to meet me. I laugh at their antics. The pigs always make me smile. I may feel unnecessary sometimes, but to them, I am the world.

I dump the feed buckets over the side of the fence and watch them greedily gobble up the pig pellets. KuneKunes are funny looking pigs. Shaggy hair, floppy ears and a rainbow of spotted colors. They swirl around each other, nudging for their food, their coats a kaleidoscope of ginger, brown, cream and black.

And dark red.

Blood.

Blood smeared on their noses, on their sides.

"Have you guys been fighting each other?" Concern and fear lick at my neck. This isn't right. They squabble but rarely fight enough to draw blood.

I climb in with them, run my hands over their thick bodies, feel for cuts, feel for lumps, feel for anything to explain the blood. They don't understand and push against me.

Blood smears on my bare legs, dark red, still wet.

Allie senses my distress and lets out a high pitched whining squeal I have never heard her make. I look through the fence and meet her eyes. Something is wrong, very wrong.

I continue searching, but everyone seems fine. They must have gotten into something. Maybe a dead deer, or a squirrel? Pigs do eat dead animals if given a chance.

That must be it, a dead deer. I take a deep breath, the pounding fear fading into a quiet drum beat. My pigs are not hurt.

The herd finishes up their breakfast and begin to wander away, taking my worry with them. I climb back out of the pasture, already planning what I need to do to remove the dead deer the pigs found.

Allie's still acting off. I stand outside the fence and watch my herd, a mother hen concerned about her little ones.

My favorite boar, Tractor, waddles his massive body over to me.

"Hey, buddy, what have you guys gotten into this morning?"

Tractor puts his front feet on the fence giving me his head to rub. Standing on his back feet, he's nearly as tall as I am. The largest of my pigs, he's also the biggest puppy of them all and loves to be rubbed. He pushes his massive head against my palm. I scratch behind his ears, careful to avoid the sickening blood staining his face. He opens his mouth, hoping for a treat.

A fingernail is wedged behind his tusk. The flag pattern expertly painted on its surface glares in stark contrast to his pale pink mouth and yellowed teeth.

I pluck the fingernail from behind his tusk, heedless of the danger of putting my hand in his gaping mouth.

The fingernail lays tattered in my dirty, blood smeared palm. I stare at it, my mind racing to make sense of the find. The minuscule red stripes and tiny white stars stare back at me.

Realization snaps into place. It's Becca's.

I haven't seen Becca since the auction. I'd wondered if she would sell the farm. My mother's instinct had worried about the bruise Ricky gave her. Mostly I have been too tangled in my web of depression to think much about her.

The blood.

The fear doesn't creep this time, it slams into me.

Oh, no. I say a prayer for a hedge of protection over Becca, knowing it's probably too late.

I sprint down the lane that runs outside of the pasture fence, headed to the woods. My bare feet slam into the uneven ground. The tall grass I had planned to mow later this week pulls at my feet, slowing me down. My breath tears, years of smoking have made me unable to run for long. My body forces me to slow, my fear pushes me to hurry.

I finally reach the woods. The gravel lane turns

to dirt and scratchy branches. The woods are silent, nothing but my wheezing breath in my ears. The fence turns into the woods here, and I leave the dirt path to follow it. Only a small part of the woods lays inside the pasture. Inside the fence, it's fairly cleared from the action of the pigs rooting. On this side of the fence, the thick summer undergrowth grasps at my legs. The brambles catch on my cutoffs, dig into my skin. The thorns draw blood that mixes with Becca's blood already smeared on my legs.

Stumbling on, I look for her. Maybe she came to pet the pigs and fell in. Maybe she's only hurt, and I can still save her.

The heavy, almost metallic smell of blood reaches me.

The scent of the blood is unmistakable, even out here in the open air. Years of cleaning and processing deer with Jackson has made the scent of blood familiar.

The smell of death.

I know that smell too.

It is close.

I fight the urge to run away and struggle along the fence line. A pile of brush rises up in the pasture, left over from when we cleared space to put up the fences. The way would be easier if I climbed over the fence, but I can't make myself do it. The fence stands as a border between me and what I know I will find. A border I don't want to cross.

I grasp the wood of the fence, desperate for air, but trying not to breathe in the horrid smell. My shirt clings in a ripple of cold sweat to my skin. I focus on the cling, desperate to focus on anything other than what I know I am going to see. I want to be anywhere other than here. I want to hear music, hear children laughing, I want to hear anything other than the incessant buzz of flies. I want to stay on this side of the fence. I want to run home and climb into bed, watch Dateline or Forensic Files. I don't want to be here.

I have to know.

I climb over the fence.

The brush looms ahead of me, a pile of horror. I follow the sound of the flies around the pile, my eyes squinting, not willing to see.

Blonde hair, so long and shining the last time I saw her, now tangled in sticks and dead leaves, dirt ground in from hooves. Becca's naked body is shoved under the branches, a crumpled mess trying to hide. She lays on her side as if sleeping. Her legs are pulled up slightly, tucked against what used to be her abdomen. A bloody tangle of entrails, blood and body parts are ground into the dirt around her, in a horrid semi-circle of death. The pigs have pulled her apart, reaching what they could under the branches. Going for the soft belly first.

I sneak closer, unable to look away, desperate to run. Becca's face peers out at me from behind the leaves and branches, an obscene game of peek a boo. Her eyes are open and stare into mine.

You didn't save me.

The side of her head is misshapen, caved in. A trickle of blood has dried in a ragged line from the corner of her mouth to her chin.

Her arms stretch out from under the brush, reaching towards me, pleading for help. One hand is missing entirely, the fingers are shredded off the other.

And the flies. The flies are everywhere, buzzing in my brain, swarming my hot face.

Screams echo through the woods. The flies rise in a sick cloud, their feast disturbed. Birds that had been sitting quietly nearby take to the air. They get to leave, to fly away. Screams tear out again. I wonder where they're coming from.

The screams are mine.

My feet realize they can run, regardless of my frozen mind. I sprint back to the fence, scramble over in a half dive. The rough wood tears along my inner thigh and I land in a hard lump on the other side. I scurry up an incline into the weeds. I claw on my hands and knees. Dirt under my fingernails, weeds scratching against my face, I am a desperate animal.

I collapse on my belly, gasping for breath. Vomit rolls in waves, explodes on the leaves in front of me. Splashes of bile and this morning's eggs splatter on my face in hot rivulets of filth. I vomit until I am empty, then roll away on the ground.

I lay there in the dirt. Sobs rip me apart. The pain sears and scars me.

I am unable to move, to stand, to think.

A cold nose pushes against me in concern, breaking into my private hell. Allie flops down next to me. I wrap my arms around her solid strength and fight to control my breathing. I feel her breathe next to me, take comfort in the familiar pattern. I match my breaths to hers and focus on calm.

"What happened to her?" I creak out in a tattered voice. Allie doesn't answer, just lets me hold her.

The initial crashing wave of panic and revulsion settles.

I let go of Allie and wipe the tears and vomit from my face with my soggy pink t-shirt. I take a deep breath, dig out my cell phone from my pocket and dial 9-1-1.

I sit on my front porch, chain-smoking as I wait for the police. I tried to call Jackson, got voicemail. He's on a long run to Colorado, spotty cell service out west. I don't call the kids, don't want to upset their world until I have to. The thought of them safe and happy far from the evil here gives me comfort. I say a prayer for a hedge of protection over my children. Not too late for them as it was for Becca. I will call them later, for now, I want them to be safe in a world they understand.

The safe world I understand is destroyed. So I smoke, lighting cigarette after cigarette, not even finishing them. The ritual of lighting them calms my nerves. My last box of smokes, it's nearly empty now. I will have to do a gas station run later. The petty concern annoys me.

I smoke, and I wait in the heat.

They come. No lights and sirens, no need to hurry. No amount of hurry will help Becca now. The police cruiser pulls in, tan car, silent lights. They turn from the street onto my driveway, breaching the protective bubble I have built around myself and my farm.

Tires crinkle to a stop in the gravel before me where I sit on the step. The Sugartree Sheriff's Department logo blazes in the sun, improbable.

I raise a weary hand in a feeble attempt to believe this is only a social call.

The sheriff climbs out of her car, shiny new uniform, shiny boots, solid gun on her hip.

"Oh, crap," I mutter under my breath. Katie Rodriguez. In my shock, I forgot she was the sheriff now. The very last person I want to see. I feel inferior, though she's on *my* property. She stands there all shiny and important. I huddle on the step, covered in dirt and blood and sweat.

"Hey, Zoey." She starts out tentatively. Or maybe I only imagine the note of uncertainty.

I pull myself together. I am a DiMeo after all, and we don't break. Not that anyone will ever see anyway.

"Katie. I mean, Sherriff Rodriguez." I try to keep the sarcasm from my voice. Small stains of sweat spread under her arms, turning dark against the tan of her stiff shirt. It makes her more human, reminds me of the young woman I used to know. I soften a little. Becca is dead, past baggage will have to wait.

"The rest of the team will be here in a few minutes. Do you want to show me where you found the body?" The body. Pretty Becca is now the body. Her choice of words ticks me off, but it's not Katie's fault, she's just doing her job.

"Becca is way back on the property. Just inside the wooded part of the pig pasture." I motion in that direction. A lovely pond and a large red barn surrounded by trees lay between us and the horror

71

beyond. The beauty of my farm seems tainted now.

"Becca? You know who the victim is?'

I crush out my cigarette and stand, ready to do what I must, but I don't answer her.

Katie's cop eyes snap at me. I am conscious of the blood on my skin.

"You can drive most of the way there on that lane. I will take the Rhino and meet you." Katie blinks, used to giving the directions, not following them.

"Okay. Deputy Watterson will wait here for the forensic team. I will drive back and meet you there." She climbs back into her car, leaving the young deputy in my driveway.

Our 4-wheeled Rhino ATV is used to the bumps and ruts in the lane, Katie's cruiser is not. I wait for her at the end of the lane, the entrance to the woods. The cruiser bounces along, its presence surreal.

"That's a long drive back here." Katie walks up to meet me, her steps strong and sure. "You found her out here?" I don't like the sound of her question. I have seen enough crime shows to know that tone.

"She's over there, under a pile of brush. Follow the fence line. It's easier to walk inside the pasture." I do not want to go near again. Her battered body is burned into my memory already, every detail drawn in permanent ink.

"How did you know she was back here?"

I don't know how to start, so I shrug. There will be hours of questions to come. Right now all I can think about is the dead young woman torn and ruined. She's beyond help but deserves better than laying in a field. The sooner the authorities can get to her, the better.

"Show me." Katie tries to hide it, but I hear the ripple of fear in her voice. I hate for anyone else to have to see what I saw, but it must be done.

We climb into the pasture together and walk towards the brush pile. Across the field, I see a few of the pigs working their way towards us. They always come to me, hoping for a treat. I welcome the excuse not to look.

"I better get them out of here." I motion to the pigs. "Don't want them to contaminate the scene any more than they have already, or get in your way. She's right over there under that brush. I rather not see her again."

"Go lock up your pigs, but stay on the farm. I want to hear everything from the beginning. Starting with why you're covered in the victim's blood."

My relief at being allowed to leave is tempered by her tone.

I am suspect number 1.

Chapter 7

I wander through my barn, trying to figure out the best way to keep the pigs away from the action in the woods. I finally rig up two lines of temporary electric fence, blocking them into a small area near the front of the pasture. A rattle of the feed bucket brings them all running into the temporary space, happy for the mid-day treat. They have been wallowing in the mud to escape the heat, and thankfully very little blood still shows on them. I, on the other hand, still have red streaks. I want to wash it off but know better than to wash anything until the police say I can. I am in enough trouble already apparently.

Yellow crime tape and official vehicles crowd the back area. My eyes are drawn to the action, but I have no interest in going back to see what is going on. Instead, I sit alone in the crispy grass along the lane absently plucking at weeds, stealing glances over my shoulder. I long for Allie, but I locked her in the house.

The coroner's van drives slowly past me, headed to the crime scene. The black van, the follower of death. Fresh tears come, sniveling and shaking. The initial adrenaline shock has worn off. With nothing to do but wait for the sheriff, exhaustion takes its place. I wish for empty, but it doesn't come. I long to lay down in the grass and just float away, to curl up like a child and cover my eyes. I am not a child. So I light another cigarette instead.

I call Jackson again. This time he answers.

"Hey, Babe." His deep voice sounds so normal, so solid.

"Um, hey." I don't know where to start. I sniffle instead.

"Zoey, what's wrong?"

"She's dead." I blurt out.

"What? Who? Oh crap, hang on. Let me pull over." I take the moment to collect myself. "Zoey, what's going on?"

"The girl I met the other day, Becca. She's dead. I found her in the back pasture. She's all torn up, shoved under a pile of brush." My voice breaks.

"I thought you meant Riley, or Allison, or even Stephanie. I don't know what I thought." His relief stings. I picture him sitting hundreds of

76

miles away on the side of a freeway, hazard lights flashing, his crying wife blurting insanity.

"The police are here now, lots of them. And of course, Katie Rodriguez is in charge, the witch."

"The police are there? I thought you meant she was in a car crash or something."

"I told you, I found her in the back pasture. Her head's bashed in, and she's all torn up. I thought maybe she had fallen into the pig pen or something, but she was murdered." The first time the word has been spoken today.

"Murdered? What, Zoey, are you okay? Who did it? Oh, man!" Jackson in a panic is a rare and scary thing. He's usually calm and in control, the rock. I shift into his customary role of protector.

"Jackson, calm down. I am fine. Okay? Everything's fine. It was just a shock finding her like that."

"Babe, I'm so sorry. I wish I could be there with you."

"Where are you?" I picture his truck on some obscure freeway far from where I need him.

"I just got into Colorado. I should be in Denver tonight to drop this trailer. I will talk to them about getting a flight home."

The child in me wants him here now, this minute. The woman in me knows that can't happen. "There's no need for that. I'm fine, really." I don't mention I am a suspect. He doesn't need that to worry about too. "The police will finish up their work and leave, and everything will be back to normal." I force cheer into my voice, willing myself to believe the sugar coating.

We sit in silence hundreds of mile apart, connected by a satellite in space. I close my eyes and imagine we are sitting together in the garage. I wonder if he's imagining the same thing.

An approaching car shatters my fantasy and breaks our silence.

"Katie's coming to talk to me. I gotta go."

"Be nice to her," he tries to make a joke. "You know she's just intimidated by you."

"I'll try, but no promises." I laugh back, not sure why I am laughing, but enjoying the feel of it.

The sheriff parks her cruiser near me and climbs out. Her face is flushed, and the sweat stains under her arms have spread. Frizzy tendrils of hair have escaped from her tight bun, and dance around her head. Her polished boots have lost their shine, and are streaked with dust and most likely manure. Her stride contradicts her unkempt appearance as she approaches confident and focused. Her eyes crack with excitement. She's on the hunt and in full control.

I have seen this look about her before. I have always been jealous of it. In a previous life, we had been friends, best friends. We spent days together riding our horses, playing in the fields, swimming in the creek, or climbing trees. By the end of the day, we would be dirty messes. She always looked amazing and assured, keyed up from our day's adventures. I always felt like a slob. That's how I feel now. Not as good.

Deputy Watterson trails behind her. He's in his late 20's, obviously new. Sugartree doesn't have much crime, and judging by the whiteness of his skin, this crime scene has been a bit much for the young deputy. I can't blame him there. To his credit, his eyes hold intelligence as they scan around him, taking in details. Even more to his credit, he doesn't know me, so he didn't arrive hating me already.

"Ok, Zoey. The scene has been processed, and the victim will be removed as soon as the coroner gets her loaded up." I flinch. Is she a piece of furniture to be loaded in a truck?

Watterson sees the flinch and gives me a tender smile. I am glad for the ally.

"Why don't you tell me what happened? Let's start with how you know the victim." Sheriff

Katie flips open her notebook as does Deputy Watterson. They both look at me expectantly.

"It's so hot, do you want to step into the barn out of the sun?" I stall.

Watterson readily agrees to the shade, Sheriff Katie reluctantly follows.

"You said her name's Becca. What's her last name?" the sheriff starts again.

"I think she said Trenton, but I don't really remember. She inherited the Applegate farm behind mine. The one that just had the auction. I guess the auctioneer would know more."

"So, you don't even know her last name. Why don't you tell me what you do know."

I light a cigarette, sit on a bucket and tell her the details I can remember from my few interactions with Becca. I don't really have much to offer. Watterson listens intently, taking copious notes, nodding along. The sheriff walks around the barn, snooping, intruding. She stops and stares at the piglets in the farrowing stall, a smile slides across her face. Scarlett grunts at her in warning. She doesn't want the sheriff near her babies, and either do I.

I finish my story with calling 9-1-1. "And then you guys got here."

"Right. We get here, and you have blood all over your legs, a large bruise on your thigh and a bad attitude."

I look at my thigh. My ungraceful tumble over the fence has left an ugly mark. I hadn't even noticed. "I told you, the blood's from when the pigs rubbed against me. The bruise I must have gotten when I went over the fence. The bad attitude you brought along with you."

Watterson's eyes open wide, and he tries to hide a smile.

"So the pigs rubbed blood on you. What about this stain here, it looks like a lot of blood." The sheriff points to a stain on the concrete floor of the barn. She is partly right, it is blood, deer blood. We gut and process deer in the barn each fall. I always joke that if a CSI team ever came to our farm, we would be in trouble. I thought it was only a joke.

"That's deer blood. See that chain hoist above you, we string deer up with that and clean them out here. You haven't forgotten how to clean a deer have you?" I snap. Katie and I used to help her dad clean deer together. We were always so proud of our skills, used to joke we could be pioneer women when we grew up.

The sheriff pulls a chain on the hoist, making it clink as the hook goes up. She doesn't say anything. I wonder if she's remembering the afternoons spent in her dad's barn, too. Two young women feeling grown up and tough. Proud of ourselves that the blood and guts didn't bother us.

Watterson breaks the silence. "Did you see anything or anyone this morning when you were back there?"

At least *he* doesn't think I am the killer.

"No. I don't think so. It was all pretty shocking." Fear tingles up my scalp. I hadn't connected the dots yet. Where there's a murder, there's a *murderer*. Becca didn't shove herself under that pile of brush.

"There was a murderer here this morning." My eyes dart around the barn, unable to focus. "Do you think I'm safe?" I lean towards Deputy Watterson and the security he represents.

"You're just fine. The murderer wasn't after you, he was after our victim. We can have a car drive by to keep an eye out if you like. Just to be safe." He looks to the sheriff for confirmation.

"Yes, that's a good idea." The sheriff spins around, heads for her car. "I think that's all we need for now. I would like you to come into the station in the morning to go over some more details and get your official statement."

"That's fine. I'll be there."

I walk them to their cruiser. Everyone else on her team has left already.

Watterson gives me a kind smile as he climbs in, I soak in it greedily. I could use a friend now.

"Thank you for your time, Mrs. DiMeo. I'm sorry you have to go through this."

"Be there early tomorrow, Zoey. And take a shower first. You're a mess." Katie slams her door and starts the cruiser.

Oh, Katie, after all these years, you're still a witch.

Chapter 8

I sit on the back porch looking over my farm. My precious, carefully crafted universe is tainted now, touched by the worst the outside world has to offer. Allie sits next to me.

Your only friend.

The light fades into dark, and the darkness fades into my mind. Bugs begin their nightly chorus.

I have nothing that needs to be done until my meeting at the sheriff's tomorrow morning. I sit, and I smoke. Empty.

Headlights break through the black of the night, cut through the black of my mood.

"Who's is here now?" I mutter, angry at the intrusion.

"Zoey?" The voice is soft and lovely, welcome.

"Back porch, Steph."

My precious sister comes around the corner of the house searching for me.

"All the lights are out, what are you doing?"

Stephanie steps up on the back porch, items in each hand.

"Just thinking." I settle farther into the patio chair.

"I am mad at you."

"What did I do now?" I don't look up at her.

"One of the nurses at the hospital asked me what I knew about the murder victim you found. I didn't know anything about it. Why didn't you call me?" Steph drops into the chair beside me, sets the things she brought on the table with a clash.

"I don't know. I didn't want to bother you." I look away.

"If you tell me one more time that you 'don't want to bother me,' I'm going to smack you." Stephanie has said this before, but never followed through on her threat.

"You know you will never smack me." I look sideways at her.

"Just kiss you, I guess." This makes me laugh. Once, when we were kids, Stephanie knocked a pile of firewood over on my feet. I was livid and raised my arm to punch her. At the last moment, I stopped, realizing I would get in trouble for hitting her.

I kissed her instead. She was so shocked, she ran into the house yelling for mom. I made my point but didn't get in trouble. The story was a familiar favorite.

"I brought you Key Lime pie. And wine. I figured you could use both."

"You figured right." Key Lime pie always makes me think of childhood trips to Florida. It's just what I need now.

I get plates and glasses, and we eat the pie in comfortable silence, listening to the sounds of the farm.

The wine and the comfort loosen my tongue.

"She was right back there," I finally say. "You can just make out the crime tape from here."

Stephanie looks where I point. "You must have been so scared." She pats my hand.

"A little bit," I say sarcastically to cover the sharp memory of the fear. I push the bloody thoughts away.

"They're saying you knew her. A young woman from Chicago."

"I met her, but I didn't really know her. Her name is Becca. Nice girl. So awful what happened to her. She didn't deserve it." The words are clichés. Sometimes clichés are the only thing to say.

"You don't deserve this either." My sister has a knack of seeing through me, especially when I don't want her to. I choose to let her see.

"Maybe I do deserve it. Maybe it's payment for my failures." I rub my legs, nervously look away again.

Stephanie is one of the few people who even come close to understanding the turmoil that boils inside me. I first started dealing with depression when we were teenagers. I was not prepared for the evil, the powerlessness. It quickly got out of hand. One night Stephanie found out how sick I truly was.

It had been an especially rough night for me. Stephanie was out with her friends, and our parents were gone for the evening.

I was alone with the voice.

The nasty words had crawled through my mind like a bloated spider spinning a web of lies. My teenage mind was no match for the evil in my head. I had no tools to fight, little to fight for.

Only pain could stop the voice.

I slammed my head into the wall, sharp and hard and fast. The pain centered me, and the spider backed away.

Another fast slam and the spider vanished.

So did my vision as I sunk to the floor.

I thought I was alone, but my bedroom door opened and there stood Stephanie, home early, unexpected.

I turned away from her, burning with shame at being caught. I hid my face, desperate to hide the truth of what I had done.

She said nothing, no condemnation, no

revulsion. She sat on the floor with me, put my head on her lap and let me cry. She stroked my back and rocked me like the broken child I was. When I was cried out, she helped me clean my face, led me to my bed and shut the door.

That night Stephanie had become my quiet guardian against an evil neither of us understood.

We never spoke of it. Even now, nearly 30 years later, it has never been discussed.

I wonder if she is thinking of that night now.

"Your failures are no larger than anyone else's, Zoey. Failure is an event, something that happened to you. It's not who you are. We all have things we regret, things we can't move past. You just have to trust it's all part of God's plan. You are learning and preparing for what comes next."

I look at her skeptically. Stephanie has never failed at anything. A beautiful, accomplished surgeon, she lives in a fancy house she designed and decorated herself. She drives the newest cars, has the latest clothes. Several times a year she goes on exciting vacations, mostly with whatever wealthy, successful man she's dating at the time. Her short-lived marriage gave her a wonderful daughter who is away at school on a full scholarship. Her life is a dream I can't even comprehend. What does she know about regret?

I am being unfair and petty, and I know it. I

don't know what to say, so I take another sip of wine in reply.

"Do you have regrets, Steph?" I finally ask.

"Of course," she says matter of factly. "I know you struggle with demons I can never begin to understand, but deep down we all have the same fears, the same issues."

A vision of the noose snaps into my mind. I toy with the idea of telling her about it, what it represents. I can't. Saying it out loud is a bridge I don't want to cross. Admitting my weakness to her will make it real.

"I'm glad you came, Steph. It has been one awful day."

"I bet it has. So, how did it go with Katie Rodriguez? You two still fighting like stray cats?" Steph takes a drink of wine, settling in for some gossip.

"I was shocked to see her. It's been years and I forgot she was the sheriff until she pulled in. It didn't go too well. For starters, she thought I killed Becca."

"Seriously? That cow." Steph sits up in her seat, full of indignation.

"I have to go down tomorrow morning and make a full statement, answer more questions."

"Like a criminal? The nerve of her. After all she has put you through?" Steph leans in close. "Want me to come with you? I have a few things

90

I would like to ask her, too." Steph's loyalty is touching.

"No, you can't come. Don't worry, I got it."

Sugartree, Indiana is like most small towns. One main street stretches lazily down the middle. Several side streets branch out, filled with small houses like leaves growing in haphazard clumps. Local businesses cluster in the center of town, flanked by industrial/office parks on each end of town. My shop had once been in one of those parks. I look the other way when I drive by.

Main Street had been a highway back in the day. Sugartree had been a nice place to stop for gas and a meal at the diner, offering a touch of nostalgia for the city people on their way to their lake cottages to the north. "Come see how the country folk live."

The new highway went in about a mile to the east many years ago. Some say that was our downfall, but I like it that way. The busy city people from nearby Fort Wayne can go wherever they want, and leave us alone. But each year Fort Wayne slithers nearer. New housing developments and shopping centers eat up the farmland and spit out progress. For now, we have managed to keep Sugartree our own, sweet as its name.

The sheriff's office shares its building with the post office. It squats ugly like most government buildings built decades ago. I sit in the parking lot watching people go about their business, dropping off packages, getting their mail. Anxiety begins to buzz, rise.

I take a slow breath, counting to four as I suck in air. I hold the breath for four then release for four. The trick I learned from Janey. I do it again, tapping out the beat on the gear shift of my SUV. The anxiety dulls.

"They're just people. You're fine. You got this."

But Katie isn't just people. Katie is the worst kind of enemy. Once close and comfortable as an old pair of jeans, now our relationship is full of sting. The betrayal a well-worn path winding through the years of our lives.

"This isn't about Robert, it's about Becca. Come on, kid, let's go."

Chapter 9

Deputy Watterson meets me in the tiny entryway. "Mrs. DiMeo, glad you could come this morning. You look better." I enjoy his genuine smile.

"Cleaner at least. No more blood." I spread my arms and look down at my clean clothes. "It was a rough night. I didn't get much sleep. I did see the cruiser go by a few times. Thank you for sending them."

"That was me," he says sheepishly. "I live out that way anyway, so I took the assignment. Not that you should need it. Like I said, the killer isn't after you. Your farm was just a convenient place to dump the body."

"Yeah, maybe too convenient." Sheriff Rodriguez interrupts. "Back here, Zoey."

Watterson shoots me a look of apology.

"Don't worry, I am used to her," I whisper.

The tiny interrogation room smells of fear, sweat and old coffee. I take my seat in a hard plastic chair in the corner. Watterson opens his notebook, Katie stands tall and hard in a fresh uniform and boots once again polished to a shine. She has full eye makeup on, mascara and everything. She even has on a hint of lipstick. Tiny changes from yesterday. War paint. I understand the need, had fought the urge to dress my best today as well. In the end, I put on long shorts to hide my nasty thigh bruise, a t-shirt, and just a little eyeliner. My usual daily dress. Of course, I do have shoes on. My feet don't like the constriction.

"As I said, it seems a little convenient that the body was dumped on your property. Why do you think the killer chose your farm?" Katie stands over me, intimidating.

Getting right to it, I see.

"How should I know?" I lean back in my chair.

"Who knows that you raise pigs back there?"

"Most of the town knows I have pigs. Nothing is secret around here, as you know so well." She flinches at the insinuation Score one for me.

"Did you see anyone around your place around 4:00 – 6:00 am yesterday morning? Anyone drive down your lane?" Watterson is determined to keep the conversation on track. "Did you see anyone in the woods or around your farm?"

"No. I wasn't up yet."

"Was Jackson there? Did he see anything?" The sheriff interupts.

"I told you, he's on a run to Colorado. He left two days ago. I was the only one home."

"So you have no alibi for the time of the murder. And apparently, you are one of the only people who even knew this girl. She was found on your property. You were covered in her blood. You do realize you are in huge trouble here." She narrows her eyes at me, enjoying herself.

"Get off it, Katie! You know I didn't kill her." My voice shakes with anger.

Watterson's pen stops scratching notes. He watches us with interest.

"I know that you like to tell lies. Maybe you are lying about this, too," Katie hisses.

"I was prepared to be professional today, but if you want to do this, then let's do it." I lean forward, ready to fight. I am tired of her threats and veiled comments. "I'm not lying now, and I didn't lie back then." I look her in the eye, my words even and clear. "I found you in bed with my husband. That was the truth, I didn't make that up." I shake inside, adrenaline spinning in my blood. Oh, I have waited years for this, ever since the day my whole world crashed.

I had left work early. Riley got sick at school, and I picked her up and took her home. Katie's car was in our driveway. That wasn't unusual in itself. My best friend since childhood, she was often at our house. But no one was supposed to be home then.

I entered the kitchen with Riley in tow. I heard noises from my bedroom. Curious, I opened the door. Robert and Katie were there, entwined. I gasped in horror, and Katie looked at me. I knew her face better than I knew my own, but I didn't recognize her then. The look of guilt and shame contorted her features. I slammed the door and hurried Riley away. Pretending nothing was wrong, I took Riley up to her room, tucked her in bed and told her to get some sleep.

I sat with Riley for a long time. I didn't want to go back downstairs. I didn't want to face what I had seen. I wanted everything to be back to normal. My life would never be normal again. I had been betrayed by the two people I trusted most. I choked back sobs, not wanting to wake Riley. I pushed the hurt as far down as I could. Eventually, I went back downstairs.

Katie had left. Probably best, I didn't want to face her. Robert waited for me in the kitchen. There were no words to say. Our marriage had been rocky for months, but I tried to hold on for Zack and Riley. There was no holding on after this, and we both knew it.

I never talked to Katie again, even blocked her number from my phone. I saw her around as you do in a small town, but we never spoke or even acknowledged each other. She never apologized.

I'm not sure I would have listened if she had. The betrayal was too deep. Some things you can't apologize for. We went on like that for ten years, until she showed up in her cruiser in my driveway.

"I trusted you! I trusted both of you," I shout now in the interrogation room.

Watterson slides his chair away from us in the small room, glances towards the door.

"It wasn't what you think! I tried to tell you that, but you didn't want to listen. You wouldn't even talk to me."

"That's a bunch of crap, and you know it. Hard to misunderstand something so simple. As usual, you just took what you wanted."

"You drove him to me," she says feebly. "He was miserable, and I was all he had to lean on."

I fly to my feet, determined. The plastic chair tumbles from my quick movement. "You are not going to blame me, Katie. We had problems, but you made your own choices, you both did." Her face is so close to mine, I can see her mascara is starting to smear. Score 2 for me.

"You cost me the election to sheriff," she seethes. "You just had to blab your mouth to everyone in town."

"You cost yourself the election! Not my fault this town found out you're a cheating whore." Her eyes hold mine, dark orbs of shock and fear.

We stand close, breathing hard, poised for battle. I wonder if she is going to take a swing at me. She inches closer, but I don't back down.

"I'm not a whore."

"You were then, and the town knew it. I didn't have to say anything."

The silence strains, crackling with anger and emotion.

She moves even closer. Her arm raises slightly, and I brace for her attack.

"Sheriff Rodriguez!" Watterson breaks in sharply, bringing her to her senses. The tension drips out of her, softening her shoulders. I raise my chin. 3 points to me.

She looks away, defeated. An unexpected rush of sympathy for her confuses me.

"You did me a favor, you know. Robert was a jerk," I say.

She gives a little laugh. "Yeah, found that out, didn't I?" Amid all the drama, Robert had dropped Katie and took up with someone else. But the damage had already been done.

Watterson clears his throat, bringing us out of the past and back to the dirty room. Katie straightens her shoulders, the scared woman replaced by the hard sheriff.

"I didn't kill her," I state.

"We'll see," she snaps hollowly, not ready to forgive and forget.

"Did you talk to the husband, Ricky?"

Katie ignores me.

"She had a bruise he gave her. Probably not the first one. Becca told me he was pressuring her to sell the farm for the money. Seems like he would be your first suspect, not me."

"Go home, Zoey. You are not a cop. Let us handle this." She rubs her neck, turning away.

"You told me to come, remember. I want to help if I can."

"Get out of here. I don't need your help." My earlier concern vanishes at her sharp tone.

"Just talk to Ricky."

Katie says nothing.

"We can't find him," Watterson chimes in. "He and his car are gone."

Chapter 10

The farm welcomes me home. I am keyed up, high from my confrontation with Katie.

I was right, she had done me a favor. Robert and I split soon after, a decision that was long overdue. We had tried to stay together for the kids, but the constant bickering and distance between us wasn't healthy for them. After the first shock and adjustment, we managed to remain friendly. We co-parented the best we could. It wasn't easy, but things were better afterwards with us.

Then I met Jackson and learned what a true marriage was. If it weren't for Katie, I wouldn't have this life here with him. The pain was worth the reward in the end.

She can blame me all she wants, but losing that election was her fault. She was young and new and didn't have much chance of winning anyway. Small towns love scandal, and when it got out, any chance of winning was gone. She thinks I spread lies and rumors, but I was too ashamed to ever speak a word about it beyond my close circle. It took her eight years, but she eventually gained the trust of the town and won.

The old scar is picked apart and raw. The first stirrings of new healing feel good. I decide to use the rush of victory and energy and put it to good use. I shove earbuds in my ears, blare music on my phone and strut across my land, purpose in my steps. Murder or no murder, I have work to do. I welcome the distraction.

The day of hard labor has worn me out. I worked on various projects around the farm, tried not to look towards the yellow crime tape fluttering across the back pasture. Now exhausted and emotionally spent from the turmoil of the last few days I lay on the couch trying to lose myself in nonsense by watching 'Parks and Recreation' on Netflix. That show cracks me up. I always laugh at how they portray the town in that show as a typical small town in Indiana. Guess those TV people in California have never been here. That's okay, it's funny anyway.

Lights pass by outside, driving slow. Probably just Watterson doing a drive-by. All the doors are locked, so I should be safe. We don't usually lock the doors. I heard once a long time ago that if you are going to be robbed, a locked door won't stop them. It gives them a reason to break the windows too. With everything going on, and Jackson still away, I locked them anyway.

I doze on the couch, not really listening to the show. I should go to bed, but it is cold and empty and holds no allure. I listen to Allie snore as always, and drift, trying not to think about the killer out there.

Allie jerks awake with a loud grunt, waking me. Normally, I wake slowly, but all my senses are instantly at attention. My pig gets up and hurries through the kitchen and towards the side door.

A rattle at that door gets my tired butt off the couch in a hurry. I am not sure where to go, what to do. Allie noses the door grunting her pig language of curiosity and interest. She doesn't seem scared, but I am.

The door rattles again, and my feet finally move to the kitchen. I should grab a weapon, kitchen knife maybe?

"Mom, the door's locked."

It's Zack. I rush to the door in relief and let him in.

"Zack, you nearly scared me to death."

"Sorry, I didn't mean to. The door was locked. I probably have a key somewhere, but you never lock the doors."

My son, comforting and strong, and so very precious. He enters the kitchen, tall and thin and not quite a man yet. I pull him close, and my head rests on his shoulder as his rested on mine as a child. I listen to his heartbeat under my ear and marvel at him. I think back to when he was tiny, and we would lay on the bed, my body wrapped around him as he napped. The memory brings tears. I fight them back, not wanting to scare him with my need.

I enjoy the moment, extra sweet in its unexpectedness, then release him.

"What are you doing here? You didn't even call to tell me." We move into the kitchen. "Are you hungry?"

"Mom recording #2." Zack tosses his bag onto the kitchen table. The kids joke that I ask if they are hungry so often I should have it as a recording. Mom recording #1 is 'I Love You'.

"I could eat." Zack sinks into a seat at the kitchen bar. "Speaking of not calling, what's the deal, Mom? Jackson called tonight to tell me what happened. You find a dead body and don't even tell your son?" He is genuinely angry, which surprises me.

"I'm fine, Zack," I say hiding my face with the fridge door as I reach to get things to make him a sandwich.

"Did you even tell Riley?"

"No." I stay in the fridge longer than necessary. Maybe I should have told them.

He makes a sound of disgust. "We're not children anymore, mom."

I don't know how to answer. I tried to call them, to tell them, but I couldn't bring myself to do it.

"I didn't want to bother you guys. I can handle it." I busy myself with making his sandwich, avoid looking at him.

But you are bothering them. You are bothering him right now.

"Crap, mom. I could have been here yesterday. I am only a few hours away. Allie, can you talk some sense into her?" he asks the pig as he rubs behind her ears.

"Here, just eat your sandwich. I don't want to fight." I walk behind him to my chair next to him at the kitchen bar. My fingers trail lightly across his shoulders the way they have a thousand times. The soft boy is gone, now replaced by hard man. I drop a kiss on his head as I sit, linger a fraction, smelling his hair. I have done this a thousand times too. When he was young, I used to drink in his smell, a lovely mix of little boy sweat and sunshine. He smells different now that he has grown, but precious none the less.

"Stop smelling me," he laughs. Another familiar joke.

"Then stop smelling so good," I say my line back, tension replaced with our customary ease.

"How long can you stay? I thought this summer semester was grueling."

"It is. I have to go back in the morning. I just wanted to see you." He takes a bite of his sandwich. "So you actually found a dead girl in the back pasture? That's wild. Tired of watching murder mysteries, decided to live one instead?" My interest, in murder shows is another long-running family joke.

"I guess so, but the reality is not much fun." Tears threaten suddenly, shocking us both.

He sets down his sandwich and reaches for my hand. "Do you want to talk about it?"

I hesitate, not wanting to burden him. I give in. "I was so scared."

"I can't even imagine." He squeezes my hand.

"I can't get the image out of my head. I barely knew her, but I liked her. And there she was, a mess of blood. I didn't know what to do or how to feel. It was awful. I don't know how to explain it."

Zack pulls me in for a hug, and I give in to the threat of tears. I have always tried to be strong in front of my kids, never show weakness, don't scare them. A brave face and a smile my usual armor. I let my armor slip and enjoy the comfort of my son for a few blissful moments.

I finally get myself back together, wipe my face on his shoulder and release him.

"Why don't you tell me about what's going on at school." I change the subject.

Listening to Zack talk is way better than thinking about murder.

I wake early, feeling refreshed and excited Zack is home. I hurry to do the chores, wanting to spend the morning with him before he heads back to school. I rush into the farrowing house and open the feed bin. The sound typically gets the pigs excited. This morning, Scarlet reacts, but Juno is quiet. I can't see her from where I am, and worry clenches my gut.

I go to her stall, expecting the worse.

Instead, a pleasant surprise greets me.

Juno lays on her side, five tiny babies are nursing. This is not the first time I have come into the farrowing house to be surprised by babies, but the miracle never gets old. They weren't here last night, and now here they are. So simple, yet so profound.

"Juno, your babies are beautiful," I say softly, not wanting to disturb her. They are still damp, newly born. They tumble over each other, jockeying for position on a teat. Baby pigs are born completely functioning. Their eyes are open, their legs work. After a few moments to get their bearings, they get up and walk around, search for a teat. It is truly amazing.

Juno rests quietly, grunts softly as she nurses. The picture is one of pure beauty. The best part of farming.

I want to share the moment with someone. Zack is still asleep, and I hate to wake him, but the babies are just too cute to keep to myself.

Back at the house, I knock on Zack's door and push it open. He is sound asleep, his face soft, his hair tousled. He looks young and adorable. I can't resist watching him sleep, a mother's guilty pleasure. He may be a college boy now, but he is still my baby.

I decide not to wake him and turn to leave.

"Mom?" I must have woken him with my watching.

"Morning, love." I feel foolish.

"What are you doing?" he rolls over, awake now.

"Juno had her babies. I was so excited, I wanted to show them to you."

"That's great, but I've seen piglets lots of times." He grabs his phone, checks the time. "Ugh, it's so early."

"I know. I'm sorry. I was just excited. Do you want to go see them?"

He rubs his face. "Not really."

"Coffee then? Since you are up already," I smile. "I have donuts."

"Well, since you have donuts."

We take our coffee and donuts out to the back porch to enjoy the early morning weather before the heat bears down later.

"We haven't done this forever," I say, sipping my coffee.

"It's nice to be home. The farm looks great. You've been working hard, it shows."

I revel in the praise. I see it every day, so I don't notice the changes. Zack's rarely home, has fresh eyes.

"Thank you, I have been working hard. It isn't easy since Jackson is gone so often. There's only so much I can do by myself."

"I worry about you spending so much time alone." Zack takes a bite of donut, a tiny smudge of frosting clings to his chin. I resist the urge to wipe it off.

"For the most part, I do ok." I take a bite of my own donut, not wanting to talk about this subject.

"It's the other part I worry about." He looks at me intently. Sometimes I swear this kid is psychic.

"It's not your job to worry."

"Yeah, it is, Mom. I love you. I don't know what I would do if anything happened to you." I

109

meet his eyes, see something there I have always dreaded.

He knows.

I hold his eyes, "Nothing's going to happen to me."

"It better not. I would never forgive you. Either would Riley or Jackson, or anyone else for that matter."

Ashamed, I look away. I don't know what to say. I swirl my coffee instead.

"Suicide is the worst sin of all, Mom. You taught me that. Your life is precious. You are precious. I know things are hard for you, but you're the strongest person I know," Zack goes on.

I'm not sure what I expected him to say, but his words surprise me.

"What do you mean? I don't do anything."

"How do you not see this? For one, you are the best mom. You went through an awful divorce, but never put Riley and I in the middle of it like some parents do. You take care of this farm almost single-handedly. You built an amazing business."

I try to interrupt him.

"I know, it's gone now, but you built it from nothing. You should be proud. And now you have this new pork business. I know it is going slowly, but you will get there when the time is right. You don't realize how great you are."

The praise sits uncomfortably with me. I am used to being my own cheerleader, not having someone cheer for me.

"Wow, that's sweet of you to say."

"Well, it needed to be said," he leans back in his chair, at ease now.

"How'd you get so smart?" I tease.

"My momma raised me right." He pops the last of his donut in his mouth.

Chapter 11

Stars swim overhead, improbable in their infinity. I take the last drag of my cigarette and toss it into the yard, the red coal dancing in the dark. The hot tub water embraces in its heat, soothing tired muscles and worn out emotions. I slide across, tip my head back until I float. Strong hands reach around me and cup my bare breasts.

Jackson is home.

I am safe.

Nothing exists except the stars above and his body behind me.

"I wish I'd been here for you." He kisses my temple, holds me tighter.

"I know, but you're here now, that's what matters." I hate myself for causing him to worry.

He pushes his lips against my temple again, breaths into my hair. He seems to need me solid in his arms as much as I need to be held. We float in the dark and the stars and our need.

"It's awful thinking a killer was so close to

you, and I was so far away."

"I'm safe now, Jackson."

"You really told Katie off? And at her sheriff's office?"

"Sure did."

"About time. You two have been at each other's throats too long."

"She started it," I giggle.

"Yeah, I guess she did. I'm proud of you."

We watch the stars, looking for satellites moving in the dark. The spell is broken, though, and I slide back into my seat.

I light another cigarette, hand one to him. We finally have a chance to talk in person, and I have things I want to say.

"I just wish I knew what was going on. Most likely Ricky did it and took off back to Chicago. It would be nice to know for sure."

"If there was anything to tell, I am sure we would know." He leans back against the headrest. He looks tired but interested.

"Yeah, right, she told me to stay out of it." I take a sip of the beer we are sharing.

"You should stay out of it. That girl was murdered. This isn't some TV show."

His offhand manner annoys me. I put down the beer, harder than I planned. It sloshes out the side of the hot tub.

"*That girl* was someone I knew. I found her. I

114

saw her all bloody and torn up." The fury I first felt laying in my puke on the hill comes back. "The killer was on *our* land. He fed her to *my* pigs like some trash. I can't stay out of it."

I stare into the dark across the property, the trees of the woods pushing into the sky. I think of Becca laying there in the still cool of the other morning. I feel the branches poke and prod my skin as they must have her skin as she was shoved under the brush. She was beyond feeling then, I feel it now in her place.

You can be beyond feeling, too. Make the pain stop.

"Zoey, don't do anything stupid."

For a moment I think he read my mind.

"Just leave it to the cops. They know what they're doing. Katie may not be your favorite person, but she's a good sheriff."

"You just don't get it." I sulk.

"You're right, I don't get it." He sits up suddenly, water splashing, and looks me in the eye. "Yes, she was found on our land, but she isn't your problem. You go poking around in something this serious and you might get hurt." Jackson rarely gets angry with me, his reaction surprises me.

"But," I try.

"There is no but. You start asking questions and the killer might come after you."

I want to tell him he is wrong, but he isn't. He just wants me safe.

Suddenly I don't care anymore. I don't want to talk about awful things or think about dark thoughts. I just want to enjoy Jackson being home.

"I'm serious." He leans closer, breathing hard.

"So am I," I say slyly, running my hand up his side.

We aren't serious about the same things.

I slide back across the hot tub and into his arms. For tonight, I just want to be lost in him. Jackson is surprised by my quick change of mood but readily goes along with my plan.

"That's not working either. Hand me the half inch."

I hand Jackson the tool he asks for, his dirty palm reaching down from where he crouches under the seat of our ancient yellow backhoe. He's been home for a few days, and we have been working on various projects that I can't do by myself. Working together, fixing things on our farm, spending hours alone together has been fantastic. The cottonwoods overhead are rattling. They don't sound like dry bones now. If I concentrate, I can imagine they are palm fronds, and we are on our own private island of sunlight.

He struggles and curses at the old machine, breaking into my fantasy of a private island. We are lucky to have such an expensive piece of equipment. It's an auction purchase from the days when we were rolling in money. It has a large scoop bucket on the front, and a long boom and a smaller digging bucket on the other end. If I squint, it looks like a strange dinosaur.

Jackson and I love doing projects together with the backhoe. He even mounted an old mower seat over the fender so I can ride next to him. We often haul brush, or wood or whatever. I sit beside him, his hand setting lovingly on my thigh. Sometimes, if I am upset and lonely, I will go out to the barn and just sit in the side seat and imagine we are doing some chore.

My favorite thing to do with the backhoe is digging holes. There's something about digging a hole and standing in it. I always feel like I am the first person ever to stand in that spot. That exact patch of land has been covered up for untold years, and then my bare feet are on it. I know it is a strange thing to get excited over, but I do.

We once had to dig a bunch of very deep holes. We were trying to locate a field tile and somehow kept missing it. We dug down as far as the backhoe could reach with its big bucket. The hole was so deep, I had to climb into the ancient bucket and Jackson would lower me gently into the hole. I would look around for remnants of broken tile, searching for pieces of the orange clay they used to make the drainage tiles. I felt like an archeologist on a dig for treasure, down in the damp hole, the smell of earth surrounding me. When I didn't find anything, Jackson would lift me back up in the bucket. We would fill that hole in and then dig another. This went on for six holes until we finally found the broken tile. It was a great day.

Another time, we were digging into the bank of our pond to get rid of some muskrat holes. The muskrats had wreaked havoc on our pond, and it kept draining into the creek nearby. We pumped as much water out of the pond as we could, then dug into the bank. We opened up a massive muskrat den. It was like a small cave. The kids were still home then, and we all took turns crawling into the den. Stephanie even brought her daughter over to go inside. The opening was just large enough to wiggle into on your belly. Farther in, it opened up around you. Roots hung from the ceiling of the cave like stalactites in the gloom. It was surreal. Luckily the muskrats were not in there, or we would have a different story to tell.

I love the backhoe, and it is fun to work with, but today it is a pain.

"I can't reach it, my hands are too big," Jackson says.

"Let me try."

He looks at me skeptically, then shrugs. I often surprise him on projects. I am not afraid to get dirty, and I like figuring things out.

We swap places.

"Is this what you're trying to get off?" I look inside the area he's working on.

"Yeah, there on the left."

I reach into the grease-covered belly of the backhoe. Black smudges streak up my arms. I can't quite touch it, so I push farther, by cheek smooshed flat against the metal body. I feel the part, put on the tool and shove as hard as I can.

It comes loose. I try to catch it, but it falls through the maze of hydraulic hoses and lands on the gravel below.

"I did it!" I smile at Jackson, hungry for his approval.

"Good job, Babe," he gives it readily. Some men might be annoyed when a woman does something they can't. Jackson's always proud of me and happy for the help.

As he reaches to pick up the loose part, I hear tires on the driveway. A Sugartree Sheriff's Department cruiser pulls in slowly, driving back to meet us by the barn.

My good feeling fades quickly. Intruded on again. Why can't the world just stay away?

Sheriff Rodriguez and Deputy Watterson walk

119

over. As usual, Katie is crisp and clean. I look down at my hands, black with grease up to my elbows. Self consciously, I push my bangs across my forehead, not thinking about the smudge I probably just left on myself.

"Hey, Katie," Jackson calls, always friendly, always open. I envy his ease.

"Jackson, this is Deputy Watterson," Katie sounds friendly and breezy, not the way she talks to me.

"Watterson, nice to meet you. I'd shake your hand, but we've been working." Jackson holds up his grease-stained hands.

"You have a lovely farm," Watterson says politely.

Katie stares at me where I stand silent on the backhoe. I don't want to come down and talk. I want them to leave. Jackson looks over his shoulder at me, a gentle hint. I climb down and walk over to them. Might as well get it over with.

Katie narrows her eyes and looks at the grease mess on me. "Zoey, looking lovely as ever."

Jackson cuts in, "So what can we do for you? Did you have a development on the case?"

"Our case is nearly closed. We're still looking into a few things, but we're certain the husband did it and took off back to Chicago." The sheriff sounds all business. "The police there are trying to track him down, but haven't found him yet.

When they do, he will be brought back for trial."

"You're sure it was him? What did forensics find at the scene?" I can't help asking her.

"We aren't able to discuss that."

I look at Watterson, hoping he has something to say. He just shrugs.

"Then why did you drive all the way out here? Did you miss me that much?" I can't keep the sarcasm from my voice.

"No. Watterson wanted to tell you personally that there is no need to worry." Katie looks away from me and focuses on Jackson. "The husband is long gone, and the case is mostly closed on our end. Chicago PD has the ball now. We were out this way anyway, so it wasn't a big deal."

"So it's over?" Jackson asks hopefully.

The sheriff nods.

"Thank God." His relief is palpable. He unconsciously rubs his hand along my back in a protective gesture.

The news is not a relief to me.

"Thank you for letting us know. And, Watterson, thanks for driving by and keeping an eye on Zoey while I was gone." Jackson is all smiles and excitement now.

"My pleasure, Mr. DiMeo." Watterson croons.

The police turn to leave. I don't move.

"Sorry about any inconvenience, Mrs. DiMeo. Everything should be back to normal now,"

Watterson says politely.

I still don't respond. He narrows his eyes for a moment, then walks away.

Jackson walks them to their car, doing all the niceties, the polite words. Katie smiles at him a little too broadly for my comfort. The tingle of anger at her interest in him mixes with the uneasy certainty I have.

They're wrong.

Chapter 12

I need smokes, so I drive to the gas station, happy to have something to do. After all the excitement with Becca, regular life feels a little dull. I hate myself for the feeling, but I can't escape it. Jackson left this morning for a five day run to New Mexico. He was reluctant to leave, but I assured him all was well now that there wasn't a killer running loose. Ricky was far away, and there was nothing to worry about.

Privately, I wasn't so sure.

I am familiar with the young woman behind the counter at the gas station. She's one of those people who always smile. Her friendliness is a welcome balm to the loneliness I am used to. I am often amazed at how the smallest gestures can mean so much.

"Here you go, darling." She hands me my cigarettes and gives me one of her dazzling smiles.

I feel compelled to talk to her, get to know her, make a connection. I don't know how.

"Sure is hot out today," I offer lamely,

embarrassed by my awkwardness. Why is talking to strangers so hard, and others make it look so easy?

"You think this is hot, you should see summers in Alabama. Whoo, Lord. Not that is hot," the woman replies.

"You're from Alabama? What made you move here?" Who knew talking about the weather actually leads to conversation some times.

"Love, darling. My husband is from here but was stationed in Alabama with the Air Force when I met him. Once he got out, I followed him here, and we got married."

"My step-daughter is in the Air Force, too." Someone approaches the counter, needing to be checked out. "Well, welcome to Indiana." I move to the door.

"Oh, honey, I been here several years now. But thank you anyway." The woman turns her bright smile to the next customer.

I watch her friendly interaction as I turn to leave, and nearly run into the young man coming in the door. I laugh nervously and step back.

"Mrs. DiMeo, how are you?"

"Deputy Watterson, I didn't recognize you without your uniform."

"It's my day off. Sorry if I startled you. You doing ok after everything?"

"Yeah, I'm good," I say automatically. The

counter girl gives a bright hello to another customer. Stepping out of my comfort zone with her worked, maybe I should step out again.

"Actually, I'm not so good. Do you want to grab some lunch and we can talk? There are a few things I want to ask you about the case."

Watterson eyes me skeptically, intently.

"I'm not sure if I should, Sheriff Rodriguez won't like it."

"It's your day off. You are allowed to have lunch with whoever you want, right? I won't tell her if you don't." My brazenness surprises me.

Watterson reluctantly agrees, and we walk across the small parking lot to the diner. I feel pretty proud of myself. I am supposed to be going out and doing new things.

We settle in a booth near the back. It's late for the lunch crowd, but I don't want everyone in the town to hear us. Once we sit, I get nervous. Maybe this is too far out of my zone.

What were you thinking? You can't have lunch with someone like regular people. Say something, you idiot.

I stare at my menu, not seeing it. Anxiety starts knocking. This was a bad idea.

It's just lunch, you loser, get a grip.

Instantly, I regret coming. I remember why I rarely leave the farm. If I am alone, I can do my tricks, fight down the panic attack. Here in this

125

booth, across from the deputy, I am stuck.

"Do you know what you want to order?" I can hardly hear him over the pounding of blood in my ears. Watterson's voice is calm and rational. The attack must not be noticeable to him yet.

You're going to lose it and make a fool of yourself in front of all these people.

"Uh, cheeseburger and fries. Can you excuse me a minute?"

My voice must sound normal because he gives no sign otherwise.

I hurry to the ladies room, desperate to escape.

I lock the door behind me, alone.

"It will pass. It will pass," I mutter to myself. "It's just a reaction, it can't last."

I lean against the sticky door, focus on my breathing.

Loser, loser, loser. Why can't you just be normal?

I don't want to hear it. I am sick and tired of that voice.

"It's not my fault," I say out loud, willing myself to believe. I do my breathing exercises.

Slowly, the adrenaline rush of fear subsides. "You got this. You got this. God's right here with you. " I repeat the words and pace the tiny bathroom until I have control again.

I turn on the faucet at the tiny sink, splash cold water on my face. The shock of the water pulls me back. I dry my face and meet my eyes in the mirror.

"See, kid. All over now. You did it." I smile at myself in the mirror, gain the strength to get through lunch. I want to go home, but I know that won't make me better. I am tired of hiding.

Watterson smiles as I return to the table, oblivious of my battle.

"I ordered for you."

"Great." I slide into the booth, back in control again.

"You said you had some questions?"

"Not questions exactly. I just have a bad feeling."

"About what?" he takes a sip of his soda.

"Do you really believe Ricky killed Becca?"

My blunt question surprises him.

"Don't you?"

"I don't know. It seems too clean."

Our food comes, interrupting. We busy ourselves with eating for a few moments.

"It is clean, that's why it makes sense," he says a few bites later.

"What do you mean?" I shove a fry in my mouth.

"I know Sheriff Rodriguez doesn't want you to know about the forensics, but they all match up to Ricky being the killer."

"I think I deserve to know what you found. I

am involved whether or not Katie wants me to be."

He gazes out the window a moment, deciding.

"There were no prints found that couldn't be accounted for. We even checked against the auction team to rule them out."

"Ok, what about DNA or something on her body?"

"She was clean. The killer must have dragged her through the creek behind your farm, washed off anything we could use. Of course, the pigs really made a mess of the scene which didn't help."

"So no prints, no DNA or anything else at the scene. Why does that make Ricky the killer? Doesn't that really mean you don't know who did it?"

"Ricky took off to who knows where. If he didn't do it, then where is he?" He sounds very sure of himself.

I eat another fry, thinking.

"I guess that makes sense. I don't know why it's bothering me. Katie knows what she's doing."

Watterson suddenly chokes on his food, startling me. I give him a few moments to compose himself. I look away awkwardly.

"The whole team knows what we're doing. You can trust us, Mrs. DiMeo," he says once he gets his breath back.

"I guess I'll stop worrying about it."

We eat in silence. I search for something to say to fill the space.

"So how long have you been a deputy?" I ask finally.

"Only about a year."

"Why did you want to become a cop?" I am genuinely interested.

"That's a long story."

"I have time." I encourage. I am supposed to be making connections.

Watterson decides to open up. "I was an only child growing up in downtown Fort Wayne. Not a great neighborhood to be a kid. My dad wasn't the greatest guy, if you know what I mean. Mom often had to call the cops to our house. I was so relieved when they would show up, know we were safe from my dad, at least for the time they were there. He finally left for good when I was ten. I should have been sad, but I wasn't."

"That sounds awful."

"For a while, things were good. As I got older, my mom tried to control everything. My friends, school, where I went and what I did. Guess she was afraid I would go down a bad road or something, who knows. It was rough." Watterson looks back out the window, focused on the past.

"So you decided to become a cop?"

"When I was sixteen, my mom fell down the stairs, broke her neck and died." He says it matter of factly, still looking out the window.

"I'm so sorry." I don't know what else to say.

"I was the one who found her. When I called the police, and they came to the house, they were so understanding, so supportive, so in control. It really made an impression on me. When I got older, I decided to become a police officer too."

We sit in silence. The sounds from the other customers and the kitchen surround us. The past sits between us.

"Where did you go then?" I stir the last of my fries, looking for any good ones I missed.

He snaps back to the present. "What do you mean?"

"You were sixteen when she died. Where did you live after that?"

"I came to Sugartree to live with my aunt. She lives out in the country by you. It was a whole world away from where I grew up."

"That sounds nice." I drink the last of my soda.

He shrugs. "It was better than what I had before."

"Does your aunt still live out here? Do I know her?"

"She retired to Florida a few years back. I bought her house when I got out of the Academy."

I reach across the table and pat his hand. "Thank you for telling me."

Regardless of my earlier panic attack, I am glad I asked him to lunch.

The waitress comes to clear our table.

"Zoey, heard you had some excitement out at your farm," the waitress says. I recognize her, but don't remember her name. Born and raised here, many people know me, but I am bad with names and faces.

"I did." I glance at Watterson, not sure how much I am allowed to say.

"I heard she was thrown in with your pigs. Did they eat all of her?" she wrinkles her nose, obviously bothered by the thought, but unable to stop herself from asking the gory details.

"If he were smarter, he would have known my pigs aren't the kind that devours everything in sight like normal pigs would." I can never pass up a chance to tell people my pigs are better than other pigs. Biased opinion, I know.

Watterson just blinks at me.

"They did chew her up enough to destroy any evidence we could have used." He is annoyed for some reason.

"Nasty business," the waitress says, gathering up our plates. "Hopefully, you guys find the jerk when he turns up," she says to Watterson.

"Don't worry, Sarah." Watterson's apparently

better at remembering names than I am. "He's long gone. Nothing to worry about, now."

Watterson looks to me for confirmation. I am unable to give it. Despite all his reasoning, I still feel wrong about it. "Sure hope you're right," I shrug.

He narrows his eyes at me in warning.

"Long gone, Sarah," I say, backing him up finally. "Nothing to worry about."

Chapter 13

The farrowing barn welcomes me in the morning sunlight as I do the chores. I check on Juno and her tiny little ones. All doing are doing well. I throw her and Scarlet their food. Scarlet's piglets are old enough to munch on some pellets along with mom. Unconsciously, I count them.

There's only six. There should be seven.

I see tiny legs peeking out of the straw in the corner, and my heart sinks. It is a simple fact of farming that not all babies make it. Sometimes they will be just fine the night before and dead the next morning. This loss hits me hard.

I reach into the pen and grab the small, stiff leg. The piglet looks just fine, no injury, not crushed, just dead. I have lost piglets before, sometimes they are even born dead. It is the way of nature. That doesn't soften the blow. I am glad I didn't bring Allie out with me this morning. She doesn't like it when I am upset.

I carry the tiny body out of the barn and across the yard to the creek. It may seem awful that I throw dead piglets in the creek. It is not because I don't care. I care very much. In the creek the little body will feed another animal, his death will not be a waste.

He is heavy and stiff in my hand. I stand on the bank and watch the water down below. I steal myself, force myself into a farmer frame of mind. I can't let it get to me.

"Good-bye, little piglet. You were loved while you were here. Enjoy piggy heaven."

I toss him hard and turn around before I see him land. I hear the splash in the water. Returning him to nature is all I can do.

I hate this part of farming.

While feeding the back pasture pigs, I see the yellow crime tape flapping in the wind. I am sick of death and sadness. The sheriff said the case was closed and my pasture is no longer a crime scene. I walk across the pasture to take the tape down. Luckily the tape is hung far enough from the brush pile that I don't have to get too close. I never want to look at it again, afraid I may see tatters of Becca still there. Jackson will have to burn the pile when he gets home.

He is on the second day of a five day run to New Mexico. Yesterday wasn't too bad without him. Lunch with Watterson filled up part of the day. The rest of the week stretches before me in a chain of loneliness and chores.

I often joke that I can walk from my barn to the house with my eyes closed since I have done it so many times. My eyes might as well be closed as I wander back to the house. I am lost in my head, thoughts tumbling, jumbling. Something just doesn't feel right. Most likely I am just upset by the dead piglet and the long streamers of yellow crime tape in my hand.

I am in a sour mood.

I shove the crime tape in the trash bin and slam down the lid.

I smash my finger in the process, suck on it angrily.

You stupid idiot. Can't even throw trash away right. No wonder Jackson is gone so much, you loser.

My mood curdles from sour to rancid.

I run my hand through my curls, pull them slightly. The tiny pain is something to focus on. I suck on my injured finger again, too hard. The stronger pain focuses me more, is welcome. Suddenly I pull my finger out and spit.

I am not allowed to do things like that anymore. Hurting myself is not allowed. I light a smoke instead.

"Socially acceptable form of self-abuse," I mutter.

Absently, I walk towards the mailbox. Maybe something interesting will be there.

Hot black top sizzles my bare feet. I fight the urge to linger and let them burn. Instead, I cross the road, grab my mail and turn. A car is coming over the nearby hill, so I pause in the gravel and weeds, waiting to cross when it is safe.

Jump in front of it, and it will all be over.

That one scares me.

The car is driving slowly but speeds up when it sees me standing there. I watch it approach, confused by its trajectory. It is coming straight for me.

Here's your chance. Just step forward.

I freeze in confusion. Seemingly against my will, I step back. The car swerves at the last moment, nearly hitting me, sliding past the mailbox instead. It's so close, the mailbox leaves a scratch the length of the driver's side. The car cuts back into the proper lane and speeds away. I try to memorize what the car looks like, the way I learned from the crime shows. I can't make out a plate number, just that it isn't an Indiana plate. The car is black and looks expensive. It seems familiar, but then it is gone over the next hill before I can be sure.

"You think someone tried to run you over?" Riley asks. I languish in the sound of her voice, even if it is from hundreds of miles away in Costa Rica. I sit on her bed while I talk to her, feeling it brings her closer.

"I'm not saying it *tried* to run me over, I'm just saying it nearly did. Probably some dumb kid who doesn't know how to drive."

"You should call Katie and tell her what happened."

"Katie is the last person I would call," I snide.

Riley is silent for a moment. I regret my words. I forget that Riley and Zack lived through all of that mess with me. Katie had been like an aunt to them. The kids never understood the anger between us. As kids, all they knew was their parents were splitting up, and they no longer saw Aunt Katie. For years it had all been behind us, now it seems to be shoved in my face again.

"Mom, let it go. I mean that in the most loving way. Some things you just have to put behind you."

I pick up a framed picture of Riley from her crowded bookshelf. It is of her at a horse show, several years ago. Her proud beauty hurts my heart. Tall and secure in her English riding breeches and show jacket, she poses with the many ribbons she had won that day. I touch the face in the picture and wonder how that girl grew into the intelligent woman on the other end of the phone so quickly.

"I know," I sigh. "It's probably nothing, though. No real need to call the police about it."

"If someone tried to run you over…."

"Yeah, *if.*"

"If you really think there's nothing to it, then why were you so worried about it that you called me?"

"It's just a feeling I have. It's all too neat. Becca gets killed, and the husband takes off. I mean, it makes sense. It just doesn't feel right. He'll get the farm now, but he can never come back and sell it, they think he killed her. He'd be caught." I warm up to the subject. I haven't had anyone else to talk to about it. Watterson disagreed with me, Jackson doesn't want to hear it and the pigs never answer. I can always count on Riley, when I can reach her.

"You said he beat her, too. Maybe that's what happened."

"But why dump her in my pig pen? How would he even know it was there? And would a city guy even know pigs can make bodies disappear?"

"You think someone else killed her?"

"Maybe? What do I know? It just doesn't make sense, is all."

"Mom, you're getting that sound in your voice.

138

Don't do anything stupid."

"Why does everyone keep saying that? I never do anything stupid," I smile, knowing we are both remembering past adventures I used to drag her and Zack along on.

"How about that time you and I went to the animal swap meet and came home with a tiny calf? It jumped out of the truck bed before we even got out of the parking lot. I had to ride home with it on my lap, and it crapped all over me," Riley laughs. The story is a family favorite.

"That wasn't stupid, that was an investment. Well, until it got so sick. Poor thing."

"How about when you took Zack and me to that old broken down house to snoop around in the dark. And that dog came after us and chased us out! Man, Zack cried the whole way home, the big baby."

"Okay, so maybe trespassing with your kids was a stupid idea, but you guys wanted to go to a haunted house, and it was sitting there empty, I couldn't resist."

I lay down on her bed, staring at the Twenty One Pilots and Fall Out Boy concert posters. This felt good, remembering and laughing with Riley. I had barely spoken to her in weeks, just occasional texts.

"Do I need to go on? I have a childhood full of kooky stuff we did."

"No, I get your point. That deserted house was fun, though." I absently run my hand along her comforter.

"It sure was." She is quiet moment, and I know her attention has turned to her present. "Hey, Mom, I gotta get back to packing. We are headed up the mountain tonight to some small villages to see their building practices, how they utilize the environment, you know that kind of thing."

I don't know. Riley lives in a world so much larger than mine I struggle to understand it.

"That sounds fun," I say absently.

"Be careful, Mom," she warns.

"What do you mean?"

"I know you, you are already thinking up something you shouldn't do. I wish I were there to go with you." Riley knows me too well.

Deserted houses *are* fun. And I have an empty house nearby that needs looking into.

Chapter 14

A summer thunderstorm blew through last night, breaking my already fitful sleep. Nightmares permeated the little rest I did get. Images of Becca's face as I last saw her battered and bloody swirled together with the images of her bright and alive. Her fast-talking words tumbled around me. One word echoed in my waking mind.

Help.

I couldn't help her in life, and I am not sure how I can help her in death. I stare at the bedroom ceiling, not sure what the dream means, or if it means anything at all. Dreams are just dreams.

"Stay out of it, Zoey," I tell myself.

I listen to my own advice and go out to do the chores. They don't take too long, and I find myself with another day stretching before me. There are plenty of projects to occupy me, but nothing that I can't postpone until later. Farm work that normally captures all my attention seems unappealing after the excitement of the last several days. I wander around the barn, Allie snuffling around my aimless feet. I absently put tools away on the tool side, straighten the small equipment we store here. I sweep out the farrowing area of the barn. Even the cute little piglets can't occupy me today.

"Oh, Allie, who am I kidding? We both know I am not going to let this go."

I am full of energy now, ready for action. I feel like my old self.

I throw some food into the extra farrow pen to entice Allie in. "Sorry, kid. You can't go with me this time." Allie eats her food and ignores me.

I hurry down the lane towards the woods. The same woods that back to Applegate Farm.

The paths cut through our side of the woods are easy to pass, and it doesn't take me long to reach the creek that's the property line between the Applegate farm and us. This time of the summer, the creek is choked with plants, and deadwood collects like piles of bones at the many bends of the creek. I carefully slide down the bank, holding onto roots and tall grasses for support. Last night's rain has everything slick and dangerous. Thousands of years of erosion has cut a deep channel through the fields and woods. At the bottom of the creek, I can't see over the banks on either side. The water is deeper than I had expected, normally barely ankle deep, it's now over my knees. For a moment I think about how foolish this is to trespass, but I am determined.

I wade across and scramble up the other side.

The Applegate farm has many more acres of woods than we do, and there are not paths cut through them. I am only vaguely familiar with the area. I have only been on this part of their property one time. A few years ago, I helped Jackson track a deer on their side of the creek.

Sometimes I go hunting with Jackson. I never carry a gun, but I like sitting in the treestand with him. We climb up in the cold dark before dawn. I don't really like ladders, and I always have to close my eyes and focus on my breathing while I climb. Sometimes I have tears when I reach the top, but I never let him know. Once in the stand, it's worth it. You can see far through the woods. The sun slowly rises, waking the woods a little at a time. It's always cold, but I snuggle against Jackson's hard body and just enjoy the time. Deer hunting is a game of patience, and I am not the most patient person. Plus you have to be quiet. Most times I fall asleep against his shoulder and wait until we can go back inside where it's warm.

This time the patience paid off and Jackson gently nudged me awake.

"Over there." He pointed into the brush. A large buck was picking his way through the sparse underbrush. His rack gleamed in the early morning sun as he sniffed the wind.

Jackson pulled his gun up and aimed with practiced skill. The pure masculinity of it excited me. Man against nature, so primal. I felt a kinship with the thousands of generations that have hunted since the beginning of time.

I covered my ears, and Jackson pulled the trigger. The deer kicked in shock and ran awkwardly away. Sometimes the deer drops a few feet away. This time it ran down the creek bed and up the other side. It disappeared into the woods.

"You got him, you got him!" I squealed, even though I know I am supposed to stay quiet. Jackson looked at me with a huge smile of pride end excitement. He looked so beautiful to me right then, it almost broke my heart. We were the only two people in the world. Just him and I way up above the ground.

"Shhh," he laughed and kissed me. "I hit him, but now we have to find him."

We climbed down the tiny ladder. I was too excited to be scared of the steps.

"Wanna learn how to track?"

Turned out we were a pretty good tracking team. I found tiny blood spatters that Jackson didn't see, and he showed me how to follow the broken branches and bent dry grasses. We eventually found the buck, and it made its way into our freezer.

The memory of that morning makes me smile as I push my way through the woods. A pang of longing slows my steps a bit. That had been a few years ago, in a better time. Jackson rarely has time to hunt much now. He's always on the road.

Your fault, your fault, your fault.

Luckily the trees thin and I am on the back part of the farm now. My attention turns from the repeating mantra to the mission I am on now.

My wandering through the woods brings me out at the far corner of the farm. The house and barns rise up off to the right, across a small field of soybeans. A tree line that divides this farm from the one next to it is on my left. That's Carter Bays' property. It's a tiny piece of land, narrow and long. His small, run-down house and few old sheds squat at the edge of the woods. Old junked out cars and trucks and tractors are parked haphazardly around.

I have never been to his property. The Bays have lived there for years. Carter inherited it when his mother died a few years ago. Jackson went there once, to look at an old truck Carter had for sale. Jackson was looking for a wood hauler, but he didn't buy Carter's. He did tell me the place was a mess. Carter goes to a lot of auctions to purchase things to re-sell. From what Jackson told me, he must not sell a whole lot.

There were piles of scrap metal and all kinds of stuff around the property. He said it looked like stuff was piled against the windows of the house, even. We like to watch the Hoarders shows on TV. Sounds like Carter is a hoarder.

From my vantage point between the properties, I can see old furniture on the front porch, a couch, a couple of recliners. I feel sorry for the person he tries to sell those to. A movement on the porch catches my eye.

Carter is there on the couch, his feet propped up on the porch railing. He raises his hand, with a bottle in it. I assume it is beer, even if it is only morning. I duck behind a tree, hoping he was just moving his arm, not waving towards me. I carefully peek around the tree. Carter's still sitting there with his feet up, looking the other way. He must not have seen me. The last thing I need is to have the little punk catch me trespassing. To play it safe, I move back into the woods to the other side of the farm. I make my way to the house where Carter can't see me.

I have driven past the Applegate farm many times over the years, but it looks different from this angle. Two large barns that had been full of equipment and tools until last week's auction sit quietly, sentries of a time long past.

A few small outbuildings dot the rest of the barnyard. The farm had always been so well-kept when the Applegates were alive. The large garden Lydia always kept has turned to weeds. Nothing planted this year. The wide yard dotted with ancient trees badly needs to be mowed now. Tall grasses clump together against the barn walls. It hadn't taken long for nature to take over once Zeke had passed away. Now no one was left to care for the old place.

Yellow police tape is still up here. No one to take it down the way I did at home. Police tape is technically an unbreakable wall. I ignore it and duck under.

I explore the empty barns first, not sure what I am looking for. Sunlight breaks through the many gaps and holes in the walls and roof, forming dancing lines of floating dust. One hayloft is still full of old broken bales of hay, covered in dust. I wander around, feeling equal measures of apprehension and futility. The police have already covered every inch of the property. What do I expect to find that they didn't?

I finish the barns and outbuildings, finding nothing more than a sense of sorrow for a time long past. I save the house for last.

The doors are locked.

Of course, they are, you idiot. The police would have locked them. Guess you didn't think that through too well.

I stand on the small back stoop, not sure what

to do, not wanting to turn back. Over at the corner of the house, they have an old cellar, the kind with doors that close flat on the ground. I stare at the doors, wondering if I dare. I look at the yellow crime tape and figure I already came this far, what's a little light breaking and entering. I won't break anything. So really it's just entering.

The doors to the cellar are not locked. No one locks up out here regularly. I swing the heavy wood back and look down. There is another door at the bottom of the crumbling steps. I expect cobwebs, but don't run into any. Small miracles.

The door at the bottom is not locked. I hesitate, wonder if I am really going to do this. Before I can think too long, I take out my phone, turn on the flashlight function and turn the door handle.

I expect a cellar packed with years of accumulated storage. It's basically empty, just a few random pieces of trash. The auctioneer did a good job. The best hidden treasures are always in the basement, tucked away and forgotten. I search the cellar, but the wooden shelves are empty. Made of old 2x4s and random sheets of plywood, they stand firm and stable waiting for future generations to fill them with new memories. One shelf leans at an awkward angle, one of the 2x4s that should hold it up is missing, and the shelf is askew. The place the board should be nailed to the others looks fresh, not coated in dust and grime. Tiny prickles of wood still stick out from the nail holes. I don't see the board anywhere. The auctioneers must have broken the shelf and tossed the board away.

I find the stairs and climb up to the first floor. Like the rest of the property, the house is mostly empty. A few dishes are on the counter by the sink. I shudder thinking Becca must have put them there, was going to wash them later. She never got the chance.

The police had already been through the house. Remnants of their inspection are obvious, not that there was really much for them to look at. Nearly everything was sold. An old mattress and a tiny TV are in the front room. Becca and Ricky had to sleep somewhere while they were here. Open suitcases are against the wall. The police had been through them too. Clothes and things lay on the floor, obviously searched. Two suitcases, one for Becca and one for Ricky apparently. In the bathroom, I find toiletries for both a man and a woman. In the upstairs bedrooms, I find nothing.

I hear a sound and freeze.

Holding my breath, I listen for someone downstairs. The vents nearby start pumping cold air.

It's only the air conditioner kicking on. I breathe a sigh of relief and decide to get out of there. The empty house and all the belongings still where they left them is creeping me out. Something still didn't feel right. If Ricky killed her and took off, why are all his things here? The question is so obvious, I'm sure the police already answered it. Sheriff Rodriguez may not be my favorite person, but she does know her job.

Discouraged I leave the house the way I came, careful to make sure the cellar doors are closed behind me. I make my way back to the woods and head home. I am not sure of the way, just head in a general southern direction, knowing I will see something familiar eventually.

The squirrels chatter overhead, birds sing all around, disturbed by my presence. I ignore them, lost in my own thoughts. I turn over the facts, try to fit them together to match the picture I was given. Did Ricky do it? He did hit her, so maybe he got carried away and didn't mean to hit her hard enough to kill. How did he get her to my pasture?

Something moves in the brush far to my right. I snap out of my thoughts, focus on the sound, frozen in place. The squirrels and birds are still making their incessant sounds. I hear nothing else. False alarm, just like the air-conditioner.

I walk on.

A few minutes later, I hear it again. Something moves nearby, closer this time. I strain to see into the trees. A deer maybe?

I want to get back to the farm. My imagination is just getting away from me, but I am ready to be back home. This whole adventure has been useless. I don't know anything that I didn't wake up knowing.

I feel I'm being watched. That tingle you can't explain that makes you turn your head in a crowd, crawls up my neck. I stop and look behind me, still see nothing. Imagination or not, the feeling beats strong.

I run.

Chapter 15

Run.

That's all I can think. I plunge through the woods, around trees, lost in my fear. I am not sure of my direction, and I don't care. Home is somewhere in front of me.

I finally have to stop, to catch my breath, bend over gasping. I look behind me, search for what chases me. I see nothing.

Nothing there, you silly girl.

I dig my phone out of my pocket, not sure who I plan on calling, but comforted by the possible connection. I still don't see anything through the thick greenery.

Something crashes behind me.

Most likely just a branch falling, I tell myself. My feet have other plans and run again.

The creek opens before me, and I hurry to cross it, the border to home. I slip in the mud, my bare feet sliding through the muck. I was careful coming across earlier, I am a wild animal now. My foot catches on a root, and I tumble forward and land with a splash, my face in the water and muck.

I can't breathe. Panicked, I push up to reach the air. The muck is thick and heavy and holds me down. The thick weeds tangle my hands. Frantic, I push hard and reach air. I suck it in greedily, still on my hands and knees, water dripping from my face.

Sharp, hot pain shoots up my leg from my twisted ankle. I don't move from my hands and knees, just close my eyes and wait for the sharp bite to pass.

As the pain fades to bearable, my senses come back to me.

I smell him before I see him.

I don't want to look, I fight the urge. Against my will, my head turns slowly.

He is a few yards away, tangled in a pile of drifted branches. It's a man, naked except for a pair of boxer briefs clinging to his waist. His skin hangs peeling and gashed. His body is bloated, a misshapen balloon animal. His head is turned facing me, purple and swollen. His sockets are dark caves, his eyes eaten by the small creek animals. His swollen lips hang open in a silent call for help. As I watch, a small crawdad crawls out and down his chin.

My screams echo down the length of the creek, bounce off the high banks. I scramble, desperate to get away. Shocking pain shoots from my ankle through my leg. The force of it knocks me back on the bank.

I have to get away, I need help.

I reach for my phone in my pocket, but it's not there. I search the bank, frantic to find it. The hot pink phone case blinks at me from the mud on the other side of the creek. I crawl to it, splashing on my knees, unable to stand on my ankle. I pull it from the mud with a sick sucking sound. Praying it still works, I turn it over. The screen is muddy, but still glowing. With shaking fingers, I dial 9-1-1 for the second time this summer.

I manage to climb up the bank to my side of the creek, but my ankle hurts too much to make the long walk back to the house. I convince myself the sounds I heard chasing me in the woods were just animals. I sit against a tree and wait. I know it will take them a while to get here. They can only drive to the woods, after that they will have to walk.

I desperately need a cigarette. The pack in my pocket is soaked. I dig into it greedily, hoping to find one that just might be smokeable. Each one falls apart in my fingers, a soggy mess. I finally find one that holds together. I dig out my lighter and spin to get a fire. Nothing. I try until my thumb is sore, then in frustration, I throw the lighter into the weeds.

The shock catches up to me. Huddled against a tree, wet, muddy, with ankle throbbing, I cry heavy wracking sobs.

When I had my shop, and the women would be talking about their problems, I used to tell them, "Sometimes all you can do is go home, lie on your bed and cry it out."

My bed now is dirt and leaves and rough tree bark, but the concept is the same. I cry until I am blurry and empty. Then lay there under the canopy of trees, far from anyone. I lay alone, don't think, and listen for the sound of the police approaching.

"Over here," I shout when I finally hear them.

I push myself back on my feet. My ankle's a little better, and I can put some weight on it. I ignore the pain and walk towards the sheriff and her team, careful not to limp.

"He's over there, down the bank." I point. "It must be Ricky." I offer.

The sheriff looks down over the bank at the body. I am watching her closely, so I see the little shudder of revulsion although she tries not to show it. For the first time, I realize this must be hard on her too. Stuff like this rarely happens in Sugartree. Nothing major has happened here since Cammie Traiger went missing. This is her first murder case as sheriff, and now it's a double.

She gives some orders to her team, then comes back to me with Deputy Watterson and his notebook in tow.

"Man, Zoey, you're a mess," the concern in Katie's voice surprises me. She looks like the Katie I remember. My friend, closer to me than my own sister, Stephanie. "Are you okay?"

"I could use a smoke," I smile, happy to be on good terms, however briefly.

Katie looks at Watterson who shrugs.

"Davis," she barks at another man on her team. "She needs a cigarette, you got any?"

The deputy walks over and offers me his pack. I snatch it greedily, take out three and hand it back. I tuck the extras behind my ears and light the welcome stick with his lighter which I keep. Today is definitely not the day to think about quitting.

"Do you want to tell me how you found him? What were you doing back here?"

I don't want to tell her. I was trespassing on a crime scene because I was nosey. No way to make myself look good in this story. There is no way around it.

"I went to the Applegate farm to snoop around," I start.

"Seriously, Zoey? You know you can't do that.

157

That's a crime scene." Her previous concern morphs into anger.

"You said you solved the case, so technically it wasn't still a scene. I took down my crime tape, so I figured what the heck."

She sighs heavily, deciding to work together. "Okay, you went to the farm and then what?"

"Well, I didn't find anything interesting, so I came home. I fell in the creek and found the body."

"You just happened to fall in the creek and find a body?"

"Pretty much." I don't want to tell them about how I ran like a scared rabbit from some noises in the woods.

"Why did you go to the house in the first place? What were you looking for?"

"I don't know. Something about this whole thing didn't feel right. Then yesterday a car that looked like Becca's tried to run me over when I was getting the mail. It started me thinking, so I went to look around and see what I could find out."

"Someone tried to run you over?" Watterson chimes in, worried. "You should have called us?"

"Yes, you should have called us, then stayed out of it," the sheriff says.

"If I had stayed out of it, you wouldn't have found Ricky," I challenge her. "And there would be a killer out there and no one looking for him."

"We don't know yet if it is Ricky," she tries, not wanting to admit she was wrong and that I helped her out.

"Who else could it be? There's still a killer out there."

She doesn't answer. "Just go with Watterson and give a full statement. I want to know everything you did and saw today," she orders then walks back to her team, purpose in every step.

"She has a strange way of saying thank you," I say to Watterson.

"Don't take it too hard. She won't like that I am telling you this, but on the drive over here, she was really worried about you. 'Poor, Zoey, first Becca and now this,' you know that kind of thing. She is afraid you are going to get hurt."

This news is shocking but welcome.

"That's a nice change, I am tired of fighting. She's not going to be happy with me when she reads my statement, though."

"Why?" he asks.

"I might have, sort of, gone in the farmhouse and looked around."

"But all the doors and windows are locked."

"The cellar doors aren't."

I wait as long as I can to call Jackson. I dread worrying him, don't want to hear the concern I cause. At the same time, I long to hear his voice, need his support. After evening chores, I sit and stare out the window, postponing the inevitable. I give in and call.

"Hey, Babe," he answers. He is happy to hear from me. I cringe at what I have to tell him.

"Hey, Love. Where are you?" I stall.

"I just got into Albuquerque."

"Really, so you are close to Allison?" This information changes my train of thought. Jackson's daughter Allison is an MP at the Kirtland Air Force base. We rarely get to see her since she joined the Air Force several years ago. She was 17 when Jackson and I got married, practically grown already. She had already decided on a career with the Air Force when I met her, and her eyes were firmly set on her future. I always regret I hadn't had more time with her before she left. Small and blonde and tough as nails, Allison is a lot like her dad, which makes it easy for me to love her.

"Are you going to see her, since you are so close?" I rather talk about the kids than the reason I called.

"Already made plans for dinner tonight." I can hear the smile in his voice. Dinner with his daughter is a very rare treat.

Don't ruin it. Let him have this night.

For once I listen to the voice. I can tell him tomorrow. I push thoughts of death and fear to the back of my mind and talk like everything is fine.

Chapter 16

My ankle is still painful and stiff the next morning. Everything is sore, my ankle, my knee, my hips, my heart. I ignore the pain and keep moving. The muscles will loosen with work. My heart will just have to catch up too. I have things to do.

I do the morning chores, feed the back pasture pigs, feed the momma sows. The routine is soothing. I am down to my last bag of feed, it won't last past tonight.

You have one job, take care of the farm. Can't you even do that right?

A trip to the feed mill is a welcome diversion. I can't focus on the farm now anyway.

I drive the familiar roads on autopilot. I think about the murders, go over all the details. Something niggles at the back of my mind, something I should be seeing. I try to grab onto it, but the thought slides away.

The feed mill rises above me as I pull in, a collection of tall silos and grain elevators that surround an old barn. It started out as a farm but now mixes feed for the many farmers in the area. I like coming here, like feeling part of the farming community. Everyone who comes here has the same concerns, caring for livestock. I am proud to be part of it.

The elevators are running, sending a gentle drift of feed particles into the air. My truck always leaves here with a pale coat of dust, but I don't mind. A few men are in the parking lot, leaning on their truck beds. It is an image as old as farming. Talking about the weather, and crop prices, maybe last night's baseball game. The things men talk about, meaningless words that bind them. I long to be part of that easy group, wonder what they would do if I walked over and joined them. Instead, I go into the office.

Shanda is behind the counter and smiles at me. I like Shanda. She is always friendly, full of sunshine. I think she enjoys my visits, another woman to talk to.

"Hey, Zoey, the usual order?" she asks.

"Yes, please." I lean on the counter.

"You are the talk of the town, you know. Finding that dead girl on your farm, everyone is talking about it. I can't even imagine." Shanda shakes her head.

"It sucked," I say lamely. Everyone talking about me? The thought is alien. No one pays me much attention generally.

"That's putting it mildly. I would have freaked out."

"Trust me, I did. And just when I got over the shock of that, yesterday happens."

She looks at me blankly. "What happened yesterday?" Guess the gossip hadn't reached her yet.

"I found Becca's husband dead and floating in my creek." I don't care if I am not supposed to talk about it. Shanda is sort of my friend and I rarely have anything interesting to say.

"No way! Tell me everything," she warms to the subject. No one else is around just now, so I lean in and tell her all about it, enjoying the attention.

"You're so brave. I would be in the nut house after something like that, and here you are just fine," Shanda says.

"I didn't feel brave at the time." The office door opens behind me, another customer coming in. "So, yeah, the usual order, please." I change the subject.

Shanda winks at me and places my order.

I wait with my truck by the loading area, the back of my SUV open, waiting to be loaded. As I wait, a shiny pick-up pulls in, "Traiger

Industries" emblazoned on its side. Bernard Traiger raises cows in addition to owning half of Sugartree, so I guess it makes sense he would come to the feed mill. I am feeling full of myself from my conversation with Shanda, and I don't want to ruin it by having to talk to Traiger. I look away. He most likely won't speak to me anyway.

A worker brings my feed in a tall stack of bags on a cart. I ignore the pain in my ankle and help him load the heavy bags. I toss the first one in and turn for another when I see Traiger approaching. Crap.

"Heard you had some excitement out at your place, DiMeo," he says by way of greeting.

"You could say that." I keep loading.

Traiger grabs one of the bags and throws it into the back. Traiger helping me? Something's up. All the bags are loaded, and the worker goes back inside, leaving me alone with Traiger.

He waits expectantly. I have no idea what he is waiting for.

"I also heard you found another body yesterday. That girl's husband." Traiger's gossip line must be more efficient than Shanda's.

"I did." I walk to the door of my truck, want to leave.

"Two bodies on your property. Kind of curious don't you think?"

"Just my dumb luck, I guess." What does he

want?

"Any idea who did it?"

"How would I know," I hedge. "You are the one who knows everything that happens in this town."

"From what I hear, you are the only one who knew anything about her. The only one who talked to her."

"Besides you."

His eyes narrow.

"What do you mean?"

"I heard you argue with her at the auction. I know you were after her farm and she didn't want to sell."

Traiger steps closer, menace in his ugly face.

"You don't know what you are talking about," he sneers. "Don't you go running your stupid mouth about my business."

His eyes are locked on mine. The eyes of a killer?

I raise my chin, tired of being bullied by this jerk.

"I heard the whole thing. Becca told me you were pressuring her, threatening her. Then she shows up dead and so is her husband. A little coincidental isn't it?"

"Coincidence is all it is. Don't get any bright ideas." He nearly shakes with anger.

"Or what?" I challenge, stepping closer.

Zoey, shut up!

Traiger storms away, leaving me shaking, amazed at my bravado.

Later, at home, I sit on the floor of the living room with Allie, rubbing her belly.

"I really did it this time, Allie. Only I would mouth off to a man who might have killed two people."

Allie doesn't answer, not impressed with my dramatics.

I need to call Jackson. He is going to be mad, but the longer I put it off, the worse it will be. I need to hear his voice. Sometimes I feel like our whole relationship is by phone anymore.

I need a smoke to get me through the call, so I go to the garage. I suck down a few drags first, stealing my nerves.

I call.

"Hey, Babe," he answers the same every time.

"Hey, Love," our ritual. "How did your dinner go?" Stalling again.

"It was great. Allison may be getting some time to come home in a few months."

"That's good," my voice sounds far away. I take another drag. The smoke my only friend here.

"Babe, what's wrong?" The sharp note of

instant concern brings tears.

I take a deep breath and tell him. The car almost hitting me, breaking into the house, falling into the creek and finding Ricky. I end with my confrontation with Traiger this morning. He listens in silence, but I can feel the tension and anger through the line.

"God damn it, Zoey!" he finally erupts. "Why didn't you tell me yesterday?"

"I didn't want to ruin your dinner with Allison," the petulant child voice again. I hate it.

"Didn't want to ruin my dinner? Come on!"

Silence again. I stand miserable in the middle of the garage.

"I'm sorry. I didn't know what to do. I mean, I am fine, so why bother you? There's nothing you can do from there anyhow." I know my excuses are meaningless.

He wouldn't be there if it wasn't for you. There are tools on the wall....

"Bother me? There is a killer out there, and you're worried about bothering me? How can you be so selfish?" the fury in his voice frightens me.

"Selfish? I am trying to make things easier for you. I can handle it." More meaningless words.

"I am a grown man, you don't have to make things easier for me. And you shouldn't have to handle it. I am your husband. I can't help you if you don't let me."

169

"You shouldn't have to help me. I made this mess, I can fix it."

Your life insurance can fix it. Just make it look like an accident, and he will get a big check.

"You didn't kill anyone. What are you talking about?" Jackson snaps.

"I am talking about our lives, the reason you are in New Mexico right now, not here with me. If it wasn't for me failing, you wouldn't have to be gone." Oh man, are we going down this road now?

He blows out air, exasperated. I instantly feel guilty. What can he do from there?

"None of that is your fault. It is just what happened. Life happens, Zoey. You can't keep looking back." I have heard these words before.

I light another cigarette, soothing myself. *"Tell him the truth,"* I think in my own voice.

I choose to trust.

"I don't know how to fix it," I say miserably.

I have said these words in therapy, but I have never said them to Jackson.

My misery softens his words. He takes pity on me.

"There's nothing to fix," he says gently. I want to believe him, want to believe it's that easy.

"Really?" I ask hopefully.

"Nothing to fix, I promise. When are you going to realize we are in this together?"

"Really?" I ask again, wanting him to repeat it, need to hear the words.

"There is nothing to fix, babe. You are not alone in this. We will get through it. You should have told me about all this before."

I am not sure if he means my guilt or the murders, probably both.

"I just picked up my trailer and am headed back to Indiana. It's going to take me a while to get back. If I push it, then maybe late tomorrow."

That feels so far away, I want him now.

"Do you want me to call Zack and have him come home again?" he offers.

"No, please don't. Stephanie asked me to go out with her tonight. She called earlier when she heard about everything going on." She had been pissed, too. Looks like I am making everyone mad today.

"So Stephanie knew before I did? Nice." His previous anger bubbles back.

"Don't be mad. It's not like I know the protocol for this stuff. I am doing the best I can." Strength in my words now.

"I know, Babe. You're doing great. Have fun with Stephanie tonight, and I'll be home tomorrow. Lock the doors, will ya."

"Already did."

Chapter 17

Sugartree only has one bar. There's not much else to do in a small town, so it's usually busy. Jackson and I don't really drink, so we never go. I sit in my truck in the parking lot, surprised at myself for going out. I wait for the anxiety to creep in, as usual. It doesn't. Guess dealing with dead bodies and murders make a night at the bar easy in comparison.

My sister, Stephanie waits for me at the bar. She is stunning and knows it. Even as I watch, a man sidles up next to her, drawn like a moth to her flame. She politely shuts him down and turns back to her drink. As always, I am jealous of her natural confidence. I guess being a gorgeous, successful surgeon gives you confidence. Being a failed businesswoman turned pig farmer doesn't.

She feels me watching her and turns with a full, genuine smile. We may be completely different kinds of people, but we love equally.

"Zoey, I can't believe you actually came out. I expected some excuse. Come here." She stands and gives me a warm hug, hanging on a little longer than normal. I sink into the embrace. This was a good idea. "Are you okay?"

"If one more person asks me that, I think I will scream," I laugh, sitting down at the bar. "I am fine, thanks."

She eyes me skeptically, her knowing sister eyes taking in every detail. I must have passed her inspection because she orders drinks for us.

"Let's go sit back in the corner, and you can tell me everything." Everyone wants to hear everything these days. I don't mind. I can tell the story again.

Half an hour and a beer later, I finish telling her all I know about the murders.

"Wow. So who do you think did it?"

"I don't know. Maybe Traiger?" My words lack conviction, not just from the effects of the two beers. "Traiger doesn't feel right to me, doesn't fit. The same way Ricky didn't fit. I feel like I am missing something."

"You're not a detective, Zoey, even if you have watched every crime show out there."

"So I have been told. Repeatedly. Man, Katie sure hasn't liked having to work with me on this. Burns her ass I found the body and threw her neatly wrapped up case in the trash."

"I bet. You guys still going at it?"

"I think we are making progress. I am ready to drop the whole thing. I mean, two people are dead, who really cares about what happened ten years ago?"

"That's a good attitude. Now, we are out here to have some fun. Let's say we do some shots."

"Shots? I can barely handle this beer," I laugh. The thought of getting lost in a haze of drink is enticing, but that's not my style. "Just another beer. You go order them, I am gonna slip into the bathroom real quick."

I return a few moments later, and Carter Bays is talking to Stephanie at our table.

"Carter was just asking me about all the action at your place," Steph says.

"It's been nuts," I say to Carter, sliding back into my seat at our booth. "Guess it has been a bit nuts for you, too. Living right next door and all. I'm sure the police questioned you. Did you see anything?" The beers have made me feel friendly.

"The police were snooping around asking questions, the usual crap they do. I didn't see anything. I stay to myself, everyone knows that." He sounds ticked off.

"Just doing their job, Carter," Stephanie chimes in flashing him one of her famous smiles to soothe him.

"They need to mind their own business and

leave me alone," he says, looking right at me. With that, he turns and walks out of the bar.

"There's something wrong with that guy," Stephanie says after he's gone.

"He's just mad at me for outbidding him at the auction. Not sure why he's so bent out of shape, it was just some old "Little House on the Prairie" books and some old comic books and stuff. Maybe he thinks they are worth a ton of money and wanted to re-sell them."

"Forget him, we came out to have some fun. Let's talk about anything else other than murder. How's the pig business?"

Stephanie knows the way to my heart, bless her.

"Going good so far. Just waiting for them to grow large enough to butcher. I really hope this new venture works out. Not sure how much longer we can make it with just Jackson's paycheck."

"Like I keep telling you, you're just being tested. If you're really that worried, maybe you should get a job." She rubs the table top. "Get out of the house, around people more."

Stop being a leach on your husband, making him do all the work.

Stephanie lives to work, is very driven by her career. My drive to make it on my own, not cash a paycheck signed by someone else has never made sense to her.

"That feels like giving up," I try to explain. "If I get a job, then I won't have time to build the new business. I will be like everyone else, stuck. I am not ready to give up yet."

"A job doesn't mean giving up." She takes a drink of her beer.

"It does to me. I feel like there's something else out there for me, and that I am building up to it. That hope is all I have. Working in an office for someone else feels like death to me. I just gotta keep working forward, soon the money will come and everything will be better, and I will be happy again."

"There's more to life than money, Zoey. I wish you would stop judging yourself by how much money you make, or don't make."

"Easy for you to say, you have tons of it," I snide. Guilt pours in the minute I say the words.

She is trying to help, and you are being rude.

"I may have money, but I don't have what you have."

"A pile of unpaid bills, a brain that doesn't work right, a failed business, a husband that has to work his ass off because I couldn't hack it in the business world. Yeah, my life is great." I take a drink of my beer to hide my embarrassment at my words.

Stephanie makes no reply, so I continue.

177

"What if I never make it big again? What if my clothing company was the best I ever do with my life? What will I do then?"

She blows out air in disgust, the same way Jackson did earlier.

"Get off it, Zoey. If you can't see how lucky you are, then screw you. Just keep on punishing yourself

Wow, this night has gone downhill fast.

Way to go, you idiot. No wonder no one wants to be around you.

We sit in angry silence. The sounds of the bar surround us. People mill about, lost in their own lives. Each one of them has something that drove them here to this bar. Each one has their own hurts and history.

She's right, as always.

"I'm sorry, Steph. I'm being selfish again." I try to appease her. She isn't in the mood for it.

"Damn right, you're being selfish. I have tried to bite my tongue, but you need to hear this. You complain that you make Jackson have to work so much. Guess what, he wants to work. He wants to take care of you and your family. All that man has ever done is support you. Your whining and feeling guilty only makes his sacrifice meaningless. Why should he work so hard if you don't appreciate it, just feel bad about it?"

She stops, surprised at her outburst.

Her tone softens as she continues.

"Be thankful you have a man to care for you. As for your business, you did it once, you will do it again. And if you don't, then so what? At least you went out and did something great. You took a chance, be proud of that. Stop focusing on yourself and your past and focus on something bigger than you."

I open my mouth, ready to defend myself against her onslaught of truth. No words come. I have no defense.

Something shifts in my mind. The puzzle pieces of anguish that I have been moving around for years finally click together. The picture they form is one of hope, not guilt. I feel lighter.

Secrets have power. The longer you keep them, the more power they hold over you. I have been carrying this guilt and shame inside for so long, it has become the center of my world. I am ready to find a new center, focus on something bigger.

"You're amazing, Stephanie," I say sweetly.

She had been prepared for a fight, not my praise. "Why's that?" she asks cautiously, ready to be back on solid ground.

"I had never looked at it like that. Thank you, I needed someone to talk sense into me, to be brutal."

"What are sisters for besides to be brutal," she

laughs. "Speaking of brutal, ready for that shot now?" Her smile is so lovely, I can't refuse.

"Just one. I'll order."

I approach the bar and order our shots. I am surprised to see Watterson standing at the bar in uniform.

"Hey, Watterson. Trouble tonight?" I look around, expecting to see a fight or something that brought the cops.

"Just picking up sandwiches. The Sheriff has us working hard now that her case has fallen apart."

Stephanie joins us at the bar. "Who's this cutie?" she asks. Steph was always a sucker for a man in uniform, but I don't trust her tone.

"Deputy Watterson, this is my sister, Stephanie."

"Ma'am." He's all business.

"So, Deputy, who do you think killed them? Zoey's been trying to figure it out." Steph moves closer than necessary to the man.

"I can't comment on the case, I'm sorry." Watterson seems nervous under Steph's interest. "It's a complicated case. Not much to go on."

"You can tell us," she leans even closer. I have seen her do this trick before. Steph is a master at getting what she wants out of a man.

"What I can tell you is that the Sheriff will never solve it. She was wrong before, and now she has no idea what to do, except send me on a sandwich run." His harsh words surprise me.

"Are you going to be able to solve it, Deputy?" she purrs. "I bet Zoey figures it out before you do."

My eyes open wide at that. Steph loves to play games, but this is too much.

"Steph, knock it off," I warn.

"Zoey's the only one who knows anything about the girl. If anyone's going to figure it out, it will be her. I'm just saying," she shrugs and turns her attention back to the bar where our shots wait.

"I'm sorry, Watterson. We've been drinking, not that that excuses her behavior." A giggle escapes my lips. I am horrified at the blunder. Stupid, beers.

Watterson is less than pleased with our antics.

"You girls stay out of trouble." He grabs his take out containers and escapes. Stephanie breaks out laughing as he walks away. I hope he doesn't hear her.

"That was mean," I say as I sit next to her at the bar.

"I don't like that guy. I've seen him around here before." She grabs her shot off the bar.

"He's been nice to me. You shouldn't tease him like that." I grab mine too.

"You're right. I'm sorry. Now, shots finally?"

"To solving the murder." We down the shots

and giggle again. I give in to the fun.

Chapter 18

After all the drinks with Stephanie, I manage to get myself home by focusing very intently on the road as I drive. Stupid, I know. I did drink several glasses of water before I left the bar so I was pretty sure I would be ok. Apparently, God was on my side this time. I make a mental promise never to drink and drive again. I sit in my truck in my driveway, too tired and ashamed to climb out. I rarely drink, now I remember why. It's fun at the time but soon fades to sick.

My stomach roils. I fly out of the truck to the grass and puke. Serves me right for being such an idiot.

The house sits quiet and dark as I enter. Allie follows me to my room. My head is clearer after my escapade in the grass, but I feel dirty and ashamed at acting so irresponsible.

I need a shower.

The hot water works its magic. I think about all Jackson said earlier and what Stephanie said tonight. Their words pour over me along with the hot water. Maybe being honest was a good thing. Maybe things will be okay after all.

Another wave of nausea comes barreling in, catching me off guard. I puke in the shower at my feet. The dark liquid mixes with the water. I imagine it's all the dark from inside me, the pain and guilt and fear. It runs down the drain away from me. I watch the filth disappear and wait for the voice to yell at me. It doesn't come.

"God's got you," I whisper to myself.

In my room, Allie starts making a racket.

"I'm fine, Allie," I call to her. Actually, I'm more than fine. I feel clearer, stronger, better than I have for years.

Allie still squeals in the bedroom. I can hear her knocking against the bedroom door, trying to get out.

I turn off the shower, throw on my robe and go check on her.

She beats against the closed door, pounding her nose into it, making quite a scene.

"Okay, okay. Give me a minute, and I will let you outside."

She darts down the hall. "Slow down, you nut." I follow her into the dark house.

Crashing comes from the other room. "I told you to slow down. What did you knock over now?" I grumble, making my way down the hall.

Another squeal, this time from a man.

An intruder.

I freeze, adrenaline pumping.

"Zack, is that you?" The late hour makes it unlikely.

No answer, just more noise.

It's not Zack.

I rush down the hall.

Chaos in the shadowy living room. A mysterious masked figure throws books off my bookshelf at Allie, trying to keep her away.

I flip on the light.

The man runs for the kitchen and the side door.

Allie follows him. She squeals in anger after the man. Her hooves scrambling on the hardwood floor, she chases the man out the side door and into the night.

I follow, entirely sober now.

The man sprints across the front yard, a shadow in the moonlight. Allie is in pursuit, the white of her feet flashing. Her speed amazes me.

Allie's fat black body crashes into the man, knocking him down. He shouts in fear and rolls on his back. Allie jumps on top of him, a wild ball of fat fury. He gives a shout of pain.

A knife flashes in the moonlight.

"Allie!" I scream running after her. She turns at the sound of my voice. The knife comes at her, slicing through the air.

She screams in pain.

I scream in fear.

The dark figure takes advantage of the moment and jumps back to his feet. He takes off down the road running at a full sprint.

Allie trots back to me, and I pull her close kneeling in the moonlit yard. I run my hands all over her, trying to find her injury. My hand comes away bloody. More blood.

I find the cut on the shoulder. Luckily, it doesn't look too bad, just superficial.

My fear and shock overwhelm me.

I hold her and cry, alone in the yard. He brought a knife meant for me. Instead, it got her.

"Allie, what would I do without you?" I sob.

Allie eventually gets frustrated with my clinging and heads for the house.

I carefully step over the broken glass from the side door. Locked doors don't stop thieves, just get you broken windows.

I go to the kitchen and get Allie a donut. She deserves it. She gobbles the whole thing down and looks at me for another, her intelligent dark eyes imploring. I give in. She did save me after all. I check her cut in the light of the kitchen. Nothing some cream and a bandage won't heal, thank god.

After enjoying the moment with my hero, I call the sheriff for the second time this week.

Katie arrives in street clothes, not a pressed

and shiny uniform, worn shorts and a t-shirt. Her severe bun now a loose ponytail. The change of wardrobe makes her more human, more approachable. She has come alone, not wanting to rouse Deputy Watterson at this late hour. We have not been alone in a room for many years. Maybe it's the lingering effects of the alcohol, maybe it's the late hour, maybe I just need a friend, but I'm glad to have her in my kitchen.

"Your pig really chased him away?" she asks after she looks around and takes her notes. "That's awesome." She looks fondly at Allie laying against the wall. My pig watches Katie wearily, ready to jump to my aid if I need it.

"She chased him right out the door and into the yard. She knocked him down and grabbed his arm. He really squalled then," I say with pride. "Then he pulled the knife on her." I shudder. "Luckily he barely got her. He went running down the road like a scared kid."

Katie looks away from Allie and back to me. "Guess pigs aren't so bad after all."

"I keep telling everyone." It feels almost like old times. Oh, how I have missed this.

The sheriff gets back to business, her notebook out again. "No idea who the man was? No idea what he was after?"

"Nothing seems to be missing. All my books are knocked off the bookshelf, but I don't know if the intruder knocked them down or Allie crashed into it. He was throwing books at her. There's nothing on my shelf but a bunch of books about farming and some mystery novels. Certainly nothing worth breaking in for."

"Have any run-ins with anyone lately? Tick anyone off?"

"Besides you?" I smile, hoping I didn't cross a line.

She smiles back. "Besides me."

"I did get into it with Bernard Traiger this morning at the feed mill."

"Traiger? What happened?"

"Nothing really. He insinuated I had something to do with it since I knew Becca. I heard him threaten her because he wanted her farm and she refused to sell."

"You accused him of the murders?" She stops taking notes, looks at me with alarm.

"Not exactly. Just told him what I knew. Then he kind of threatened me," I finished.

"Threatened you how?" her eyes narrow.

"Keep your stupid mouth shut, you don't know what you're talking about, that kind of thing. Besides, Traiger's too fat to run like this guy did."

Katie shakes her head. "Zoey, you sure have a way of falling into trouble."

"I don't mean to. I just stay here on the farm

and want everyone to leave me alone. I don't go looking for trouble." I busy myself with filling glasses of iced tea for us.

"Isn't breaking into a crime scene house looking for trouble?"

"Watterson told you?" I ask sheepishly, handing her a glass, not sure if she will accept it.

"Of course he did." She takes the glass and sits next to me at the kitchen bar. "But since the deed's already done, did you see anything that might be helpful?"

"You mean, did I find something your team missed?" I can't help rubbing it in a little.

Katie sighs, "Yes, that's what I mean. I have two murders and now another break-in. I can use all the help I can get. Did you see anything unusual?"

"Just that the cellar doors aren't locked. That might be how the killer got in, through the cellar."

She makes a note in her book. "Anything else? Anything you haven't told me."

The slipping thought floats just beyond my grasp. I still can't get a handle on it. "Nothing I can think of. I have been racking my brain, but I've got nothing."

We sit in companionable silence, each sipping our tea. The fridge kicks on, a quiet whir.

I get up the nerve to ask the question I have

been avoiding.

"Do you think he came here to kill me?"

Katie doesn't answer right away. "I don't know. It may not even be related. Could be a robbery attempt. He had a knife, and Becca and Ricky were beaten to death, not stabbed. Killers tend to stick to one method. He could just be trying to scare you. Or maybe it's some kid looking for money. There was a break in last week, could be related."

She grasps at straws, and we both know it.

"We really have no idea, do we?" Defeated, I sip my iced tea.

"No. I wish I did. I have been over it and over it, but nothing pans out. Even Traiger's alibi checks out for Becca and Ricky. We have no suspects, no clues. I don't know what we're going to do."

"Katie, I know we've had our problems, but you're a good sheriff. You will solve the case." I want to be supportive.

"We never solved the Cammie Traiger case." She sounds defeated.

"You weren't in charge of the Traiger case," I point out.

"No, but I worked on it. Now here's another case I don't know how to solve."

We listen to the whir of the fridge, neither of us knowing where to go from here.

Allie huffs from her place on the floor, breaking the spell.

"I'll send the forensic team by in the morning. Hopefully, they can find something."

Katie finishes her tea and stands to leave. "When does Jackson get home?"

"Tomorrow night." I stand too, suddenly hesitant for her to go.

"You should go stay with your sister tonight, to be safe."

"There isn't much night left anyway, so I will stay here. No one scares me off my farm. Besides, I have Allie."

Katie shakes her head kindly. "Some pig," she says, quoting the movie we both loved as kids.

"Yes, she is."

Katie walks to the side door, and steps over the broken glass. "The team will be here in the morning. For now, get some rest."

"I will. Hey, Katie?" she pauses at the door, question in her eyes. We made progress tonight, but a wall still stands between us. I push the wall down.

"Why did you never call me after?" I have wanted to ask for years, never had the nerve.

She thinks about her answer. I worry she will make some snarky remark, and make me hate her again.

"Guilt makes us do stupid things, Zoey," she

says softly, kindly. Not exactly an apology, but from Katie, it's as close as I will ever get. I accept it easily.

"Thank you."

We both know I am talking about more than her police work tonight.

Chapter 19

The forensic team arrives early as Katie promised. They've been to my farm so often, I am starting to recognize some of the members. What a strange way to make friends.

I stand out in the driveway while they do their work, unwilling to witness their intrusion.

A sheriff department cruiser pulls in. Deputy Watterson climbs out and hurries over to me.

"Mrs. DiMeo. I can't believe this happened to you."

His presence calms my nerves. "Hey, Watterson. Seems you guys can't stay away from here." I attempt a smile. "I'm glad you came."

"I should have been here last night, but Sheriff Rodriguez didn't call me in. I just found out this morning."

His concern is touching. "That's okay, Katie handled it. Not much to see, anyway. It was all over so quickly."

"Your pig chased him off, is that right?" He looks around, expecting to see Allie with me as usual.

"She sure did," I say with pride. "She's locked up in the barn right now. All these people around were making her nervous.

"I know you already talked to Sheriff last night, but do you have anything else to add this morning?" He flips out his ever-present notebook. I wonder absently what they do with all the handwritten notes. Put them in a computer somewhere I imagine.

"I really don't know anything. The man wore a hoodie, face mask, and gloves. He was fit, probably young. I really couldn't tell anything about him. I was more concerned about Allie at the time."

"So no idea who it was or why he was here?"

I shake my head. "He must live close by or had a car close. He ran away on foot."

Watterson flips his notebook closed.

The forensic team comes out with their equipment bags. "All done," one of them says to Watterson.

"Thanks, guys."

The team drives away, leaving me alone with Watterson.

"Most likely just a break in, not related to the

other things going on," Watterson says, hopeful.

I let myself believe that last night.

"That's what Katie said, but it doesn't make sense. We've never had trouble out here before. Seems a little too coincidental." My harsh tone catches him by surprise.

"Some things are coincidence, Mrs. DiMeo."

"None of this makes sense. Does it make sense to you? This farm used to be my safe place, now it's a crime scene again. Why can't you guys figure this out and make it stop?" The strain finally breaks me. "He came here to kill me. We both know it. But why? I never did anything to anyone."

I cross my arms across my chest, fight frustrated tears, stare at the ground. I don't want to cry in front of my new friend.

Watterson reaches out, raises my chin gently. "We will find him, Mrs. DiMeo. Trust me. You don't know he came to kill you, maybe he was looking for something. Maybe you know something, or he thinks you do. Either way, you need to stay out of it. If he thinks you have info on him, he won't stop till he stops you. You should have stayed out of it like we told you."

"I tried to stay out of it and look at what happened. Would you stay out of it?"

"I would listen to the police. We know what we're doing."

"Ricky didn't do it. Traiger apparently didn't do it. Who does that leave? Becca didn't know anyone else here. Some random guy?"

Watterson doesn't reply.

Suddenly, I remember something Becca said at the auction.

"He was sure I was out with some other guy. I told him I only know one person in this town, and I definitely don't want to see him."

"Wait, she did know someone. She told me at the auction."

Watterson perks up, interested in this new information.

"Why didn't you tell us this before?"

"I forgot all about it. At the time, I was more concerned that Ricky hit her."

"Did she give a name?" he flips out his notebook again.

"No. She just said she didn't want to see him."

"So, no idea who she was talking about?" Watterson closes his notebook, disappointed.

"Had to be someone she met when she was here before." I'm still missing something, it skitters out of my mind.

"If you think of anything, call me."

I am only half listening, my mind scrambling.

"I will figure it out. I promise you. I owe Becca."

"Let me know if you do."

My head hurts from last night's drinking. I need Tylenol. I down the pills at the kitchen sink, look over my familiar farm.

What I really need is Jackson.

I pull out my phone, and we go through our ritual hellos.

"Someone broke in last night," I finally say.

"Are you kidding me? I don't know how many more of these phone calls I can take. I should have stayed home with you like I said," his anger crackles across the line. I let him talk, knowing he isn't mad at me but at the situation. "I want you to go stay with Stephanie or go to a hotel, I don't care. Just get out of there. Damn it, I should be there!"

His anger unsettles me, not sure how to soothe him.

"It's okay, Jackson. I am fine now," I feel like I am having déjà vu, I've said these words so often lately.

"It's not okay. I feel useless so far away. I should be there with you."

"When you left, there wasn't anything to worry about. You didn't know. Besides, you will be home tonight." Home tonight, I can't wait.

"I should be there now," he says quietly, guiltily. "Does Katie have any idea who it was or what they wanted?"

197

"No. He messed up my books, but Allie interrupted him." I tell him about Allie's heroic actions

"Super pig, huh?" he laughs.

"I tell you, don't mess with a protective pig. That guy's lucky he got away. She was pissed." It feels good to laugh with him.

I take "super pig" with me out to the barnyard. I have let things slide a bit the last several days, and I am anxious to get back to work. I have several hours to fill until Jackson gets home. I welcome the busy work to fill the time.

I don't want to think about murder and break-ins and knives flashing in the moonlight. I want to think about farming and baby pigs, and gourmet pork sales coming in a few months. Empty feed bags are piled high in the barn, giving me an idea. A large pile of trash and brush back along the lane behind the barn waits to be burned. Today's a good day for a fire.

The empty feed bags light quickly, and soon the whole pile of brush and trash is engulfed. I love burning trash. Fire is cleansing. Piles of useless stuff disappear, leaving room for something new. I stand back and watch the flames lick the sky, the smoke rises in a dark funnel. I think about my conversation with Stephanie last night. I imagine the burning trash as the trash in my mind I have been holding onto the last few years. I am ready for it to burn away and leave room for something new.

I close my eyes, lean my head back and open my arms to the sky, open myself to the wonder of the universe, to God. I imagine all my troubles and battles and fears rising out of me, disappearing with the smoke. I feel good, reborn, ready for tomorrow. It has been a long time since I have felt this way, I feed on it greedily. I deserve the moment of peace.

Suddenly, the vague prickle of someone watching me intrudes on my private moment. I open my eyes and look around. I am alone.

The spirituality of the fire fades leaving a pile of burning trash again. I head back to the barn carrying the new lightness with me. The feeling of being watched follows me, too and I can't help but look over my shoulder down the lane. Nothing.

I clean out the barn, trying to occupy my mind. Thoughts of the murders and break in play over and over, but won't click together. The cleaning keeps my hands busy and occupies a few of the hours at least.

I clean the farrowing pens out and throw in fresh straw. Leaning over the low wooden fence, I scratch Scarlett behind the ears. That missing piece bubbles in my thoughts then slips away again.

"Oh, Scarlett, why can't I remember what it is?" I ask the sow.

Remember. Remembrance Book.

"I fancied that someday I could be a writer like she was. I even started keeping a 'remembrance book,' you know. Like Laura did. The silly things a 15-year girl does," Becca had said at the auction.

I have to find the box I bought at the auction. The Little House books were in the box, maybe her journals were too.

"That's it, Scarlet!"

I rush to the house, then stand in the kitchen, lost. What did I do with the box?

I go over my steps from after the auction. We usually bring auction items inside the day we buy them, anxious to see our treasures. We had so much fun together on auction day, our version of a romantic date. When we got home, we were focused on each other, not boxes of old things. The memory of our evening makes me blush even now.

The box must still be in the back of my truck.

I run back out the side door to the driveway and find the box in the back seat of my SUV. I toss the box on the kitchen table. There really isn't much in it. The "Little House" books, of course, a couple other young adult novels, a few old letters and postcards, and a few old comic books. The kind of things you find in a drawer or on a shelf and throw together. I start to give up hope of finding anything interesting. I flip through the comics, shake them out for good measure.

A spiral bound notebook slides out and lands on the floor.

I snatch it off the floor and open it.

Chapter 20

Childish handwriting that can only be Becca's fill the pages.

I take the notebook to the living room, settle on the couch and read.

"If I had a remembrance book, I would write down what happened to me this summer. So far there hasn't been anything to write about. My parents shipped me here to Indiana to stay with my grandparents. They said it would be a good experience for me, I think they just wanted me out of the house for a while. They fight a lot lately.

"Indiana's not too bad. Nothing like Chicago where I'm from. It is very quiet here, and nothing much happens. Grandma and Grandpa are great. They seem to enjoy having me around, like teaching me things about the farm. It seems strange dad grew up here. There's nothing to do.

"Another day of quiet farm life. Grandpa did let me drive the tractor today, that was cool. He said he might let me drive the old pick-up truck even though I don't have a permit yet. That sounds fun.

"I helped grandma pick green beans in the garden. She has a huge garden. I asked her why she didn't just buy green beans at the grocery like everyone else. She found that funny for some reason. Old people.

"I did see a guy next door today. He seemed about my age. Wonder if he is as bored as I am or if he is used to it.

"Talked to mom tonight. She sounded tired. Hope her and dad are getting things figured out.

"Grandpa was true to his word and let me drive the old pick-up today. We just went up and down the road, but it was great. I can't wait until I get my license for real. Then I can go somewhere.

"I mowed the yard today. We don't have a yard in Chicago, so it was a first for me. It was so hot, I wore my bikini top to get a tan. That guy next door must have liked it, I saw him watching me. He looked kind of cute. I wish he would come over and talk to me. I've been texting my friends back home, but it would be nice to have someone to hang out with here.

"Well, I guess some things do happen around here. Everyone is talking about some girl named Cammie Traiger that went missing a few months ago. She was about my age. It's kind of creepy. In Chicago, things like that happen all the time. I thought it would be safer here. Hopefully, she just ran off or something, and will show up just fine.

"Dad called tonight. He sounded tired too. I wish they would hurry up and get this figured out. Or at least tell me what is going on. I am 15 now, I can handle it. Doesn't seem fair to send me away and then not tell me the whole truth about the situation. I want to ask them, but I don't for some reason. Maybe I can ask grandma and grandpa about it. If they wanted me to know, they would have told me already, so maybe not. I wish I had someone to talk to other than this journal. That guy next door seems promising. I feel him watching me a lot when I am doing things outside. If he would just come talk to me, that would be something. Maybe guys here aren't as forward as they are back home.

"Neither Mom or Dad have called the last two nights. Hope they are figuring things out. I'm so sick of being here. I love grandma and grandpa, but I miss Chicago. Nothing happens here! I can only entertain myself with chickens and fields and thing for so long.

"I actually have something to write about tonight! Today I saw that guy next door out in his yard. I figured if he was only going to stare at me from afar and not talk to me then I would talk to him. So I walked over. I was right, he is cute. His name is Neil. We had a nice talk. I told him about Chicago, he told me about his job cleaning buildings for some place called Traiger Industries. He is older than I am, but not too old. He didn't come out and say it, but I think he likes me. We talked for a long time. It was nice. Hopefully, I can see him again tomorrow.

"I have been busy the last few days, so I haven't had time to write. My new friend and I have been spending a lot of time together. We went for a walk in the woods today, and he held my hand. His hands are strong and rough from working. I liked how my hand felt in his. I wish we could go out to a movie or something, but I get the feeling grandma and grandpa wouldn't let me go. Everyone is so worked up about that missing girl. I guess here it's a big deal.

"I didn't get to see Neil today, so it was pretty dull around here. I did get to go with grandma to Wal-mart. Sad that is the highlight of my day.

"Talked to both mom and dad tonight. They sounded better than they have all summer. Hopefully, this time alone is doing them some good. I haven't been too alone. I spent the day at Neil's house, watching TV and talking. He lives with his aunt. I don't think she liked me very much. She barely said anything to me all day. She just kept watching us like we were doing something wrong. All we were doing was hanging out. Oh well, Neil likes me plenty to make up for it. He keeps telling me how pretty I am and how important I am to him. It's nice to have someone pay attention to me. I told him I was keeping a journal now. Maybe tomorrow I will let him read some of it.

"He kissed me! Wow, my first kiss. It was so wonderful. We went for a walk in the woods again. He took me to what he called his "special place." It was this place in the creek back in the woods. Kind of like a rocky cove or a branch in the creek or something. It was very secluded. The banks reached so high over our heads, it felt like we were the only people in the world. We sat on a big rock and talked and laughed. He was telling me how much he likes me and how glad he is I came into his life. He said he wouldn't know what to do without me. Then he leaned in and kissed me! It was so romantic! Definitely not going to let him read this journal now.

"He kissed me again today. Actually, he kissed me a lot. We were in the woods again, at his special place, and we started kissing. It was great at first, but then it got weird. I don't know how to explain it. He got carried away and a little rough. Maybe that is just what guys do. Either way, I didn't like it and told him to stop. He did stop, so I guess everything is fine. Maybe we should stay out of the woods for a while, so it doesn't happen again. I don't want him to get the wrong idea. Hopefully, I am going back to Chicago soon, so I don't want to get too involved. It might be different if I was living here, but I'm not.

"I didn't see Neil today. That's okay. I am kind of mad at him still for yesterday. There was a big news story on about that girl that went missing a while ago. They still haven't found her yet. Her dad was on TV asking for help to locate her and bring her home. Breaks my heart, I feel so sorry for him. I can't imagine. My parents sent me here, but at least they know where I am and that I am safe.

"Today was a bit strange. Grandma and grandpa were gone, and I was here hanging out by myself. I went outside, and I found a note taped to the back door. It was from Neil. Why would he leave me a note when I was obviously home? It was a weird poem. All about how beautiful I am and how much he wants me. How he lays awake at night thinking about me. I suppose it was meant as flattering, but it wasn't. I will have to ask him about it tomorrow.

"I asked Neil about the poem he left me, and he said it was something he copied out of a book and thought I would like. I didn't like it, but I didn't tell him that. If he didn't actually write it, I guess it doesn't matter. We sat on the back step together tonight and talked. He told me how his parents are gone, so he lives with his aunt. I felt so sorry for him that I forgave him for the odd poem. He seems as lost as I am. I am glad we have each other.

"Good news, my parents said everything is worked out now, and I can come home in a few days. I can't wait to go back to Chicago. I don't want to have to leave Neil, but we can still text and talk on the phone. I miss my real friends and my apartment with my parents. I miss the city. I get to go home!

"I don't know how to write this or even if I should. I don't have anyone else to talk to about it. Tonight Neil came over, and we went up into the hayloft to hang out. I hadn't told him yet that I am going home tomorrow. We kissed for a while, and it was sweet like usual. After a while, I had to tell him I was leaving tomorrow. He got super mad and just flipped out! He said a bunch of stuff like 'How can you leave me, I thought you loved me, I can't live without you.' I was terrified. I tried to calm him down, and at first, it seemed to work. Then he asked if he could kiss me. I wanted to make him feel better, so I let him, even though I didn't really want to kiss anymore. It was nice at first, but then he pushed me back on the hay and wanted more. I tried to push him off me, but he just kept kissing and grabbing and getting carried away the way he did in the woods that time. I told him to stop, but he wouldn't. He just got angry and rough. He started to pull at my clothes and beg me to let him have me before I left. He said he needed me. He said I was the only one who could save him. He said he thought Cammie could save him but that she didn't, she wasn't innocent enough and I was. He was talking crazy and didn't even look like himself.

I was terrified. He pulled my shorts down, and I was sure he was going to rape me. I fought as hard as I could. Just then, Grandpa came out to the barn to get me for dinner. Neil just froze. He looked me right in the eye and said if I told anyone what happened or what he said about that other girl, he would kill me and my grandparents. I was so scared, I just nodded, sure he meant it. Then he climbed out of the hayloft and left me there. I don't know what to do. I go home to Chicago tomorrow. Maybe I can just pretend it never happened. But what about that missing girl? Should I tell someone about it? He said he would kill my grandparents if I told anyone. After seeing that look in his eyes, I believe him. I just want to go home and forget all about him."

The abrupt end to the journal snaps me back to the present. I flip through the remaining pages of the notebook, hoping to find out more. They are all blank. Between the very last pages, a piece of paper is hidden. The handwriting is not Becca's.

It's Neil's poem.

At night I watch you sleep, peaceful and precious
I burn to touch you but don't dare to wake
My need for you is the food of my soul
I hunger to fill myself with the self of you
I long to possess, to hold you closer until we are one
I must take your innocence to drown the evil void

I can see why Becca was so upset by the poem. I throw the diary and the poem on the floor, soiled from reading it.

Who is Neil?

I look through the box, hoping to find a clue.

Several unopened letters are in the box. Addressed to Becca at her grandparents. The return address shows Six Mile Rd., the same road as Applegate Farms. The return name, Neil Watterson.

Deputy Watterson.

Sick betrayal thrums through me.

I hurry to the kitchen to where I left my phone on the kitchen table, looking for the card Katie had given me with her direct number as I go. I have to tell her.

I smell smoke, stopping me in mid-stride.

211

I run to the window and look out back. Smoke rises from the barn, at first I think it is just smoke from the burn pile I lit earlier. Red and orange light dances behind the windows. It's not the burn pile.

My barn is on fire.

Chapter 21

My brain has room for only one thought, reaching the barn and saving the pigs. I run through the gathering dark, panic moving my feet. The baby pigs are in the fire. I have to save the babies.

Nothing can scream like a pig. Their screams tear across the yard, piercing me to the core. I can't run fast enough, I push harder.

After an eternity, I reach the barn door, throw it open. Flames are crawling up the walls, thick smoke burns my nose. Scarlet and Juno are screaming along with the babies, panicked. They claw up the fences, trying to jump over.

The heat sears my bare skin, the smoke chokes. I push inside anyway. I hurry to open the gates, my fingers fumble in my terror. I finally get Scarlet's pen open, and her massive body pushes past me, knocking me down against the wall. Tiny bodies follow, scrambling over my legs, scratching me as they run for safety.

Juno and her babies are still screaming, my ears ring. I can barely breathe as I crawl to her gate. I fumble with her latch and throw it open.

Ready for her charge, I jump out of the way. Tiny, week old babies follow her out into the barnyard and scatter into the night.

They are safe.

The old wooden barn is fast fuel as the fire crawls along old beams and reaches the hayloft. In a whoosh, the hay lights. I think of the hose, and run to get it. I know it is futile, but I have to try. The hose is at the back of the barn, near the tools. I scramble around the tractor, climb past the backhoe. I am almost to the hose when an explosion knocks me back. The fire has reached the gas cans. The hulking frame of the backhoe shields me from the blast.

It's no use. The barn is lost.

I turn to run back out the door, eager for fresh air and cool. I reach for my phone. It's not in my pocket. I was headed to pick it up earlier but never did get to it.

I cough and gag my way through the smoke. I see the open door, safety. Just a few more steps.

A hand grabs my arm, a rope wraps around my neck.

"You should have done what I told you and minded your own business. " I can't see his face, but recognize Watterson's voice. "I thought Becca had a journal. When I saw you reading it, I knew you would ruin me." The voice crackles with menace, barely recognizable as the kind deputy I know.

The rope tightens around my neck as he pulls me back into the barn. I fight and strain, but he over-powers me. I lift my legs, trying to throw him off by the sudden change in my weight. The rope only gets tighter, and he doesn't let go.

"Nice try. You are not my first struggling woman."

The sound of chains rattles among the crackling flames. He lets go of my arms, and I try to make a run for it. The rope around my neck pulls me back. I claw at it, need to escape.

"You won't get away. They will find you burned and hanging, and think you killed yourself. They will have no idea. I will be here to process the scene. That will be so sweet." His voice drips with excitement. "The Sheriff will be so upset, too. Ooh, I can't wait."

"Jackson will kill you." I force bravado into my voice.

"Becca thought the same thing. Ricky just whimpered and ran into the woods. I had her all to myself."

More chain sounds. He's tied the rope to the chain hoist we use for deer. Slowly, the rope tightens, raises. I stand on my toes, trying to be taller. My heels lift. I turn my head, trying to find a looser part of the rope. There is none. Just the tips of my toes touch the concrete now. I scramble, trying to reach the floor. The floor disappears.

I am hanging.

"It's sad, really. I liked you. It has been fun watching you. I will miss that. Maybe I should lower you just enough so I can have a taste of you before you die."

He runs his hand up my bare thigh, sickeningly slow. I kick him will all my strength. The movement causes me to swing, the rope grows tighter.

"I like it when they fight back." He croons. His hand returns to my skin, I force myself to stay still, not give him what he wants.

His hand slides up my shorts, violates. I close my eyes to the inevitable.

Across the barn, a beam lets go, crashes down in a cascade of sparks, the flames increase.

Watterson jumps at the sudden sound.

"Better at starting fires than I thought," he chuckles. "I wonder," he takes my hand, strokes it lovingly. "So rough, so strong. A nice addition."

I struggle to pull my hand way, he clamps on my wrist, pulls my hand to his mouth. My fingers slide into his mouth. He sucks, eyes closed in revolting ecstasy.

Another crash, I manage to pull my hand away.

"Ooh, if only. But it would give me away."

Watterson eyes the growing fire. "Looks like our time is up."

He pushes my body. I swing in a sickening arc as he walks out of the barn.

He's left me hanging in the fire to die.

I cling to the rope with my hands, trying to pull myself up, fighting for air in the smoke. Heat presses on me, smoke chokes me. Nothing exists but the rope.

Just give in. You wanted this. Now is the time.

The thought comforts, entices.

My dim mind focuses on images of those who love me. Riley and her bright smile, Zack and his precious hugs, Jackson and his quiet strength, Stephanie and her undying loyalty.

They will think I did this, think I failed. Blame themselves.

Lack of oxygen blurs my thoughts.

Like a flash, one clear thought.

I want to live.

I will win this battle.

Like a physical presence, I feel God fighting along with me.

I struggle to focus. What are my options? I am hanging from the chain hoist. That means the fences are next to me.

With the last bit consciousness left, I swing my leg for the fence of the farrowing pen. Bare toes grab the top rail, clinging. I pull myself closer to the fence, just enough slack in the rope. Somehow I get my feet under me enough to soften the bite of the rope. I can breathe the hot smokey air.

I claw at the rope again, can't get it off. The chain hoist rattles above me. I reach for the chain, praying I don't lose my grip on the fence. My fingers wrap around the links, close on the hot metal. I pull, chain clinks through the gears. More slack in the rope.

Link, by link, I pull. The hoist lowers me in agonizing slowness. I balance on the fence, fight for breath. The flames have taken over the whole barn. The heat burns, my will to live burns brighter.

The smoke and heat are the enemies now. I fight panic. I want to jump from the fence and run, but I know I don't have enough slack yet. I focus on the chain, nothing but the chain and its excruciatingly slow clinking.

My vision blurs, I shake my head to clear it and keep pulling. The chain has lowered the rope quite a bit, is it far enough I can reach the ground?

The smoke wins, and I lose vision, lose my balance. My nightmare come to life. I grip the fence with my toes. My legs buckle, and I fall.

I hear the chain above me. It's clinking fast now, too fast. As I fall, I realize I am not pulling the chain. The sound makes no sense.

I brace for the bite of the rope.

It doesn't come.

Arms surround me. I fight them, sure Watterson has come to finish me off. All my will to survive and he will win anyway. I push.

"Zoey, it's me. Stop fighting."

Jackson.

I collapse on the concrete. The air clearer here, I gulp it greedily. Jackson shoves his arms under mine, drags me to safety.

"Stay with me, babe. Stay with me, babe," he repeats over and over. I focus on his words. Jackson has me, and I am alive. Nothing else matters.

He drags me from the heat and the smoke into the night. The heat of July cools my scorched skin. He lays me down under the giant cottonwood trees. A flash of knife glints orange in the flames. I don't flinch, I trust Jackson will never hurt me.

The knife pushes against the skin of my neck, slides under the rope. One strong slice and the rope slides away.

I gasp, finally able to breathe normally. Clear air enters me, the first breaths of my new life, sweeter than any breath before.

Jackson gathers me close, shaking from his own terror. I sink into his safety. He pats my hair, rubs my back, touching to assure him of my wholeness. We cling together under the tree while our barn burns and crackles nearby.

It's just a barn. I am alive.

"I thought I lost you," he murmurs into my hair. "You scared the hell out of me. Why did you do it, Zoey?"

"I didn't do it. He tried to kill me."

"You didn't do this?" he asks hopefully.

"No, I didn't. I would never do that to you." He slumps against me, relieved.

"I thought," he doesn't finish. "Wait, who tried to kill you?"

"Deputy Watterson. He killed Becca and Ricky, and Cammie Traiger."

Suddenly, I snap out of my daze. Watterson tried to kill me, and he is nearby.

"Do you have your phone?" I sit up, excited.

"Zoey, what's going on?" He pulls his phone from his pocket.

"Call the fire department, call the police" I jump to my feet, ready to fight.

I run for the house.

"Where are you going?" he hollers, confused, his phone already to his ear.

"Be right back. We need the Rhino. It will be faster."

Chapter 22

I jump into the Rhino and throw it in reverse. I pull out of the garage and fly back to Jackson by the burning barn. I focus on him, not the barn. We will deal with the barn later.

I skid to a stop and jump out.

"You drive, you know the trails better than I do." I run to the passenger side.

He still has the phone with emergency dispatch on the line.

"Just drive to the creek, we will have to walk from there. Here, give me the phone."

"This is Zoey DiMeo," I tell the dispatcher. "Tell Sheriff Rodriguez to meet us at Deputy Watterson's property. He killed Becca and Ricky and tried to kill me."

"Your husband already told us. Sheriff Rodriguez is already in route, ma'am."

"Send the fire department to my address. My barn's burning down.

"Yes, ma'am. Fire is already in route too," the dispatcher says.

I look at Jackson, thankful he already took care of it.

I hang up the phone.

"Are you going to fill me in now?"

I explain about Becca's journal and the letters as we fly down the lane to the woods.

"So I was going for my phone to call Katie to tell her Watterson was the killer. That's when I saw the barn on fire."

We crash down the paths in the woods, the Rhino bouncing over ruts and downed branches. I hang onto the roll bar to keep from being bounced out.

"So I got the pigs out. Oh yeah, where are they?" I shout over the sound of the Rhino and crashing branches.

"Zoey, the pigs will be fine. What happened to *you*?"

"I got them out, and then Watterson grabbed me and strung me up. He said he wanted you to find me and think I killed myself."

"I got home, saw the flames and knew you would be there. When I saw you hanging, I did think you did it. Another minute or two and you would be…"

"It wasn't another minute or two, Jackson. You got there in time." I squeeze his hand reassuringly.

We reach the edge of our property and pull the

Rhino to a stop. The creek blocks our way.

"Ready?" I should be scared, but excitement strums instead. With Jackson beside me, I can do anything.

"What's the plan?"

"I don't know. Watterson can't be too far away. I was only in the barn a few minutes before you came even though it sure felt longer. He was on foot, and we had the Rhino. I'm guessing he went back to his house."

"Let's go," he climbs out of the Rhino.

I expected him to tell me to stay out of it, wait for the police. I can tell by the set of his jaw he wants the man as badly as I do.

We creep through the woods, our senses on high alert. Little chance Watterson knows we are coming. He thinks he killed me and doesn't know Jackson came home. The threat of being ambushed in the dark makes every night noise sound ominous. Each cracking branch or rustling leaf makes me jump. Jackson plunges on, unfazed and determined.

Jackson knows these woods much better than I do, and before long, we are at the back of Watterson's property.

I have driven by this house but never been on the property. From our vantage point in the woods I can see Applegate Farm clearly, and Carter Bays' property on the far side.

Trees and a few large sheds surround the single-story house. No lights shine from the windows, and the house gives off an empty vibe. Disappointment washes heavy over me. I was sure he would be here.

"Let's check the house." Jackson motions to the back door.

We pick our way across the back yard, using trees and sheds for cover. At the back door, we hesitate. I don't think we'll find him here, but have to be sure. Jackson reaches for the handle and turns it.

The door swings open, silent on well-oiled hinges.

We look at each other, gaining strength, then enter.

The scent of cleaner lingers in the air.

The kitchen gleams back from Jackson's cell phone flashlight, pristinely clean. It looks like no one actually lives here. No stacks of mail on the counter, no dirty dishes in the sink.

We search the rest of the house, ears straining for movement or footsteps. Silence is all we hear.

The bedrooms have no dirty clothes on the floor. The beds are made up, blankets pulled tight and smooth. Towels in the bathroom hang in perfect alignment.

The house small house doesn't take long to search, and we wander back into the kitchen.

"It's so clean, do you think he even lives here?" Jackson breaks the silence.

I open the fridge. Fresh food inside, lined up neatly. I slam the fridge in disgust. No sane person would live like this.

"Fresh food. He lives here."

We stand in the sterile kitchen, not sure what to do next.

"Let's check the sheds," Jackson suggests.

We check the sheds one by one, each organized to perfection. Tools hang neatly on the walls, lawn equipment lined up in exact lines. I get the same creepy vibe from the sheds as from the house. No rational person keeps things this neat. After experiencing Watterson's true self first hand, the insanity of his home doesn't surprise me.

We save the largest shed for last. Inside we find a car with Illinois plates. Becca's car. A long scratch runs down the driver's side.

"So he did try to run me over," I shutter, running my finger down the length of the scratch from my mailbox.

Not sure what else to do, we close the shed door and go back outside.

"He's not here. Now what?" Jackson asks.

I stand confused. Ready for battle, but no

opponent. Where would he go? His car sits in the driveway out front, so he has to be here.

"Applegate Farm," I say suddenly. "The scene of the crime."

A quick walk brings us to the backyard of the farm. The dark house gives off the same empty vibe the other house did. The uncanny certainty no one is inside.

Jackson and I look at each other and shrug.

A small sound bounces across the yard from the largest barn.

We both look towards the sound. "He tried to rape Becca in the hayloft." I hurry to the barn. Jackson doesn't question, he just goes with me.

The barn looms in the barnyard, the door an open mouth of darkness. We sneak inside.

A rustling sound comes from the massive hayloft. I was right.

"They're going to find you. You were careless this time. No, I wasn't. They will think she killed herself. I did it right." Watterson is talking to himself.

Built-in ladders flank each end of the hayloft, barely visible in the moonlight filtering through the access window in the peak of the barn. Jackson motions to me to go up one, and he will go up the other.

I hate ladders but block out the fear. I climb as quietly as I can. Watterson lost in his anguish doesn't hear us.

I reach the loft and climb up. I can hear him, but I can't see him in the gloom.

He hears me.

"What the hell?" he exclaims.

"It's over, Watterson," I say.

"You should be dead," he hisses.

"Well, I'm not."

He moves into a small beam of moonlight, his face streaked with tears and grime. Behind him, Jackson climbs into the loft. Watterson doesn't notice.

"You came back to finish what we started, didn't you? Want a little taste after all."

The man before me is so far removed from the friendly Deputy I knew it seems impossible they are the same person.

"What happened to you, Watterson? You seemed so nice before." I want to keep him talking.

"That puppy dog? He's so easy to manipulate. Has everyone fooled, though. I'm just the nice deputy everyone trusts. Good cover, don't you think?"

"What I think is that you're sick."

A board creaks under Jackson's weight, giving him away.

Watterson whips around.

"So you brought back up."

Bales of old hay are stacked up high around us, a towering pyramid. Watterson talks tough, but he starts climbing up the bales, away from the menace in Jackson's face.

"What's wrong, Watterson? You only like to pick on women?" Jackson asks, following Watterson up the bales.

"I can take you." Watterson tries to sound tough, but his hasty climbing shows his cowardice.

I climb behind Jackson up the hay bales ready to help him if needed.

Watterson faces us both, fear in his eyes now. He scrambles higher. The stacks of hay bales reach almost to the access window. A short wooden ladder leads from there to a small platform. When loading in the hay, a lift pulls the bales from a trailer outside up to the window. Men unload the bales into the loft, standing on the platform.

"How dare you hurt my wife." I have never heard this tone from Jackson before. It stirs something primal in me.

We keep climbing, moving in on our prey like stalking animals. Watterson reaches the ladder, climbs to the platform.

Jackson follows, calm, in control, intent on his

target.

I trail right behind, caught in the spell.

The two men stand on the platform, facing off, breathing heavy. I wait on the ladder, watching over the edge of the platform.

The sound of sirens approaching cuts through the quiet. Blue and red lights dance through the window and swirl on their faces.

Watterson looks toward the sound, realizes all is lost.

He suddenly lunges for Jackson. Jackson anticipates his move and shoves him back. Watterson teeters out the window, grabs Jackson's shirt to steady himself. The momentum of the push carries him out the window, taking Jackson with him.

I scream and dive to grab Jackson.

My hand claws down the bare skin of his leg and finally closes on his boot, stopping his fall. Outside the window, Watterson's scream fades as he falls.

I cling to Jackson's boot as he hangs head first, halfway out the window. I pull him back to the platform. He manages to wiggle back in the window into my arms.

The sirens are loud. The lights bounce into the barn from the property next door. They are at the wrong house, but it doesn't matter now.

"Man, babe. That was close," Jackson says into

my hair, crushing me to him.

The sirens blare, but Jackson's heartbeat under my ear blocks everything else out.

We cling together, relief flooding my veins.

"We probably should go tell Katie," I finally break the spell.

Jackson doesn't respond, just holds me tighter.

"Is he dead, you think?" I don't want to look. I have had enough of dead bodies for a lifetime.

Jackson looks over the side of the barn.

"I don't see him," he says surprised.

I look too. A pile of old straw is below the window, but no Watterson.

"He's gone!"

Chapter 23

Jackson and I stare in disbelief at the empty ground. We look at each other, confused. Then hustle down the ladders and out of the barn.

Jackson's cell phone flashlight reveals a dark red stain of blood, but no Watterson. He scans the area, looking for more blood. A few drops lead in a track towards the woods.

"He took off," Jackson says.

"But we had him," I whine. "We had him. He fell."

"I don't know, babe. He can't get far, judging by the blood trail."

I grab his phone and call emergency dispatch. Katie and the other police are still at Watterson's house, I don't have time to walk over there and tell them what happened.

"Tell Sheriff Rodriguez Watterson's hurt and took off into the woods. We're going to track him from here. Have her follow."

"Ma'am, you need to let the sheriff handle this," the dispatcher says.

"I am not stopping now! Just give her the

message, damn it."

I hang up on her. I am sick of people telling me to stay out of it. He killed my friend, he burned my barn, he nearly killed me then tried to kill Jackson. I want the bastard.

We enter the dark woods on quiet feet. Watterson could be waiting for us, ready to attack. Jackson uses his light to look for blood, holding it low to block the light. A spot glimmers on a leaf. We fan out searching from that spot until we find the next. We stop often, listen to the night for sounds of his movement.

Jackson and make a good tracking team. The dark makes it harder, but we have tracked in the dark before. Granted, that was deer, and this is a killer, but the procedure's the same. Look for blood, follow broken branches, bent grasses.

The spots of blood get closer together, a sure sign of increased bleeding.

We stop again to listen. Crushing brush gives Watterson's position away.

"That way," Jackson points.

Far behind us, I hear Katie and her team. We're being as quiet as possible, not wanting Watterson to know where we are. They're making a huge racket. We hold our light close to the ground, hiding its beam. Their flashlights cut through the dark in long lines of white light. I hope he will focus on them and not know how close we are.

The trail leads to the creek and down the bank. We slide down and land with only a tiny splash. We lose the trail in the water, don't know which way to go. We stand and listen to the night. Splashing sounds come from the right. He's in the creek bed, moving upstream.

Jackson and I hurry in pursuit. The steep banks rise above us on either side, blocking out the moonlight. We struggle through the water, stopping every now and then to listen, to make sure Watterson's still in the creek.

No more splashing sounds. We look at each other, not sure what to do. Did he climb out of the creek?

I strain to hear anything. In the distance, the sheriff's team is still making noise, closer now. I can hear nothing else but the slow trickle sound of the creek, the hum of night insects, the whisper of the breeze in the branches.

A low moan.

My head snaps in the direction of the sound. Jackson follows my gaze. Up ahead, there's a branch of the creek, like a cove. It must be the place Watterson took Becca to in the journal.

We approach cautiously, not wanting to scare him into running again. The banks here are very high, and steep. We block the entrance.

Watterson sits on a large rock.

Jackson turns the flashlight on him. He flinches from the light but ignores us.

He rocks himself like a child, clinging to something clutched to his chest, lost in his private hell.

I approach him cautiously, Jackson close behind me.

"Zoey, no," Jackson tries to grab my arm. I shake him off.

I have to see.

"I'm so sorry, Becca. I'm so sorry Cammie," Watterson mutters.

He senses my closeness, looks up, his face a horrid mask of blood.

"What do you have?" I ask gently.

He proudly holds out his treasures for me to see.

Hands. One a skeleton. One rotting, flag fingernails still attached.

I scream.

He doesn't respond to my scream, just holds out the hands looking for approval.

Watterson looks me in the eye. The pain and guilt there drowns me. He lost his battle with the dark. I am filled with sorrow for the loss.

"It's okay, Watterson. It's okay," I try to soothe him. He is beyond soothing.

My scream drew Katie and her crew to the top of the bank. Flashlights pour over us from above. I don't turn to look at them, I focus on Watterson.

The small part of him clinging to reality fades as the flashlights illuminate us. He lunges for me, dropping the bones.

Jackson swings and punches Watterson with a satisfying crunch. Watterson flops on his belly in the dirt. He lays there beaten, whimpering into the soil.

"Let's get out of here, Zoey." Jackson has no pity for the man. "Katie, come arrest this ass."

Jackson looks up to where the police stand on the bank. As he turns his head, Watterson springs up with a rock in his hand. He slams Jackson in the head, and he crumbles to the creek bed, limp.

I try to go to Jackson, but Watterson pulls me away. He crushes me against his chest, his arm across my throat. His ragged breath blows across my ear. The intimacy of the moment disgusts me. I kick my legs, try to escape.

"I'm going to kill you for sure, this time."

He raises the rock. I have no time to move away, or even scream.

The rock rushes at me in a swift arc.

A gunshot rings out, echoes off the banks. My ears ring from the sharp sound.

Watterson goes limp, slides away from my body and drops at my feet.

I look over my shoulder. Katie stands on the bank, her pistol in her hand.

I step over Watterson's dead body and rush to Jackson's side. I put my ear to his chest, desperate to hear the familiar beat.

It thrums strong and sure.

Katie slides down the bank and kneels along with me.

She checks his head wound with her experienced cop hands.

Jackson moans and tries to get up, ready to protect me.

"Stay still, love. Everything's okay now. We're just checking your head wound." I place his head in my lap, smooth his hair. Behind me I hear a deputy confirm Watterson is dead and another call for an ambulance for Jackson.

"It doesn't look too deep, but you are going to have a nasty headache for a while." Katie rocks back on her heels.

Jackson is more awake now. "What happened?"

"Katie shot him." I look at my friend. I don't have the words to thank her.

She just nods, reading my mind like we did as kids. She pats my shoulder and stands to get back to work.

"You got your killer, Katie." I call after her. "He killed Cammie Traiger too, and probably his own mom."

Her eyes ask questions but her mouth says, "We'll talk tomorrow. Now, you and Jackson get to that ambulance. Let us handle it from here." I am only too happy to let her take over.

Jackson gets to his feet, a little unsteady, but otherwise ok.

He stares at the dead body of Watterson. The hatred nearly sizzles off of him. I can't make out his expression in the dark, probably best. I don't think I could bear seeing that hatred on the face I love so much.

I don't feel hatred for the man lying in the dirt. I feel sorrow. We all have demons in our heads. Some demons are stronger than others. I am familiar with the battle. My personal devil turned against me, tried to destroy me from the inside. His devil destroyed others. The distinction is so fine, I don't want to face it.

"Let's go home." Jackson turns me away from the body to face him.

"Ambulance first. Make sure you're ok." I brush my fingers across his brow and trail them down his cheek. His slight stubble grazes my fingertips.

He pulls my hand away and kisses my palm.

"Smoochy kiss?" Jackson asks. We both laugh,

the release of nervous tension making our voices too loud.

He squishes my cheeks and kisses my pushed out lips. The familiar endearment grounds me.

We climb together up the creek bank.

"We need to get the Rhino," I say. It feels like hours since we left the Rhino in the woods.

"And round up the baby pigs." He adds.

We reach the top of the bank. Far away through the woods, we can see the police lights at Watterson's house. Farther way, towards our farm, we can see the lights of the fire trucks.

"Our barn." I look at Jackson, feel the worry etched on my face.

"We'll build a new one."

Katie calls up to us from where she is working. "I'll talk to you tomorrow, Zoey. You guys need some help getting back?"

I look down at my friend, then back at Jackson. "Nope, *we* got it."

238

If you enjoyed this debut novel by Dawn Merriman, please leave a review on Amazon.

You can also follow Dawn Merriman on Facebook or at DawnMerriman.com to find out about new releases.

Follow the story of Zoey and Jackson DiMeo in the sequel coming out summer of 2019.

Made in the USA
Middletown, DE
25 April 2019